Weep Not for Me

Book One: The Stranger

Weep Not for Me

Book One: The Stranger

Mary Sturlaugson Eyer
Author of: A Soul So Rebellious

This book is not an official publication of The Church of Jesus Christ of Latter-day Saints. All opinions expressed herein are the author's and are not necessarily those of the publisher or of The Church of Jesus Christ of Latter-day Saints.

Published and Distributed by:

Granite Publishing and Distribution, L.L.C.
868 North 1430 West • Orem, UT 84057
(801) 229-9023 • Toll Free (800) 574-5779
FAX (801) 229-1924

Cover Art by: Maureen Heagany
Production by: *SunRise Publishing, Orem, Utah*

ISBN: 1-890558-65-6
Library of Congress Catalog Card Number: 99-95471

Foreword

These things I have spoken unto you,
that in me ye might have peace.
In the world ye shall have tribulation;
but be of good cheer; I have overcome the world.
—John 16:33

I hope I can share this fictional story as Ms Mamie and others in this piece of history would have shared it. But, if words should fail me, may the Lord's Spirit successfully communicate the trials and triumphs of the great love and faith of those individuals involved. I am grateful to be an instrument in His divine hands in seeking to unfold a story of an extremely challenging road to His true gospel.

—*Mary Sturlaugson Eyer*

vi

Table of Contents

Acknowledgements

My mom always said that you could judge the strength of a friendship by the severity and number of storms it endured. My life has had a lot of difficult turns lately. I am most appreciative to those who became a steady anchor before, during, and after each storm, especially Randy and Patti Sims, Syd Seitz, Peggy Roland, Maxine Thompson, Bruce and Debbi Brown, Bert Wilmore, Annalee and John Strong, Mollie Gulsby, James and Norinne Thorpe, Bruce and Jean Thurston, the Barlockers, Glen Roundy, Ray and Judy Howes, Kaye Stout, the Dinkelmans, Jan and Cliff Spendlove, Rev. France Davis, the Drapers, Stan and Barb Cox, Bishop Kacher, June Strong, Judge Mike Dobson and Bret and Roberta Stark. I am especially grateful to my daughter, Tai. For her unconditional love and support, I am blessed. The true gospel of Jesus Christ truly maketh my cup runneth over.

Molaire wrote, "The greater the obstacle, the greater the glory in overcoming it." Below, I introduce the world to a group that has truly challenged me, taught me, and profoundly enriched my life. These are the true heroes of the millennium.

To each of them, I express a heartfelt thank you. I am confident that they will be instruments in the Lord's hand in making this world a place He would be proud of: Matt Hassler, Jaci Davis, Cameron Gordon, Danny Gardner, Kandi Klein, Andrea Torre, Brian Brown, Emily Johstoneaux, Lyndsie Olsen, Erin Wilson, Nate Phillips, Emily Wilson, Rory

Williams, J.R. Lindsay, Matt Clarke, Christine Lund, Jake Bryson, John and Bekah Luke, Sean Knudsen, Jason Snelson, Shiloh Lundahl, Shiloh Blair, Sae Joon Kim, Gabby Ortiz, Jamie Hammond, Adam Famulary, Kara Purcell, Eric Nielson, Ashlee Eyre, Liesl Legorburu, Melissa Merrill, Josh Byrd, Aaron Darais, Lindsey Robinson, Camilla Dinkins, Janalee Davis, Andy Stutz, Jodi Peterson, Josh McKell, Anna Lewis, Ronald Ortiz, Rachael Johanson, Chris Ohran, Peter Brown, Maureen Heagany, Melissa Lyon, Sam Harrison, Hannah Edsberg, Anne Kimball, Elizabeth Loosle, Chris Hill, Jenny Doria, Mike Moore, Virginia Reay, Ed Watson, Chantel Cooper, Ray Johnson, Kerri Russell, Whitney Ridenour, Scott McDaniel, James Davis, Leslie Reim, Amy Peck, Emily Foerster, Justin Griffith, Uillame Bell, Neomai Iongi, Jenny Tomlinson, Vanessa Sorenson, Amanda Majors, Amanda Pearson, Laura Keller, Kristine Livingston, Angela Bradford, Grant Salmon, Catherine Taylor, Jenny McCoard, Leslie Christiansen, Whitney Christiansen, Steve Stone, Jennifer Fuentes, Diana Yanez, Tommy Zane, Ben Boekweg, Gini Stringham, Ryan Hatch, Jeff Larsen, Jordan Hoopes, Jonny Payne, Andrew Dalton, Holly Porter, Brent Wilson, Clint Curtis, Nicole Messick, Ammon Jones, Matt Humes, Justin Huntington, Tiffany Brodbeck, Craig Mackay, Jimmy Kim, Justin Anderson, Olof Heide, Sharla Coston, and Heather Grover.

"Greater love hath no man than this,
that a man lay down his life for his friends."

Her name was Mamie, but people had always called her Ms Mamie. She didn't remember much about her youth; either the memories were too painful, or they were not worth remembering.

A poor way-faring Man of grief
Hath often crossed me on my way

Chapter One

The Stranger

Mamie smiled as she busied herself making bread with the few cups of cornmeal given to her by her Massa. The day had been an extremely challenging one as they tried to clear a field to make it usable for a cotton crop, but Mamie's smile grew broader as she thought about how one of the younger boys working in the fields had ended the day by giving them all a hearty laugh when he tried to ride home on a stray dog.

The boy complained about being too tired to walk and, since no one was willing to carry him, he got the witty idea to ride the dog. He innocently coerced the animal to him and then hopped on its back. All the field hands stood watching and waiting to see what would happen. The dog stood perfectly still as the boy straddled it, wrapped his small arms around the dog's neck and then yelled, "git gon' doggie, git gon'." He yelled at it four or five times with absolutely no movement from the animal. The kid, becoming restless, removed his arms from around the dog's neck, sat up straight and yelled, "Yous dumb dog; yous too dumb to know how to *git.*" Immediately, like a flash of lightning, the dog shot forward, leaving the boy still sitting in an upright position on the ground.

Mamie still wasn't sure whether it was the look on the boy's face or the position he was left in, that had been the funniest. Her smile gave way to a peaceful feeling as she thought about the laughter and how good it felt after a hard day's work in the sun. She looked forward to getting together later that evening with the rest of the slaves to sing praise to the Lord.

Mamie turned to check on her eight year old daughter Ruth and again smiled. For a brief moment she watched the child playing quietly near the opened doorway, left open to feel the warmth from the last rays of the evening sun. As Mamie turned and continued making the bread, she did not hear the man's knock. She only heard the panic in her child's voice when she said, 'Mama.' With fear racing through her heart, Mamie instantly turned. As Mamie did, her heart surged with fear, and she gasped loudly. Just outside her door stood a tall white man.

With her heart beating nervously, Mamie rushed to shield her daughter from him. Pushing the child hastily behind her, Mamie stared at the stranger. She could feel her child trembling behind her and sorrow ripped through Mamie's heart as her eyes clouded with tears.

"Good evening, ma'am," the stranger smiled and said as he removed his hat.

Mamie frowned at him, unable to believe her ears. Most slave buyers were loud and arrogant when speaking to slaves. Saying 'good evening' or 'good' anything to a slave was unheard of. This man smiled, called her 'ma'am', and even removed his hat. Mamie felt Ruth leaning slightly from behind her to look at him. The stranger extended one of his hands toward the child.

"Please, don't fear." he said.

Ruth quickly ducked behind her mother from his view, although Mamie noticed her child was no longer trembling.

As Mamie continued staring at the stranger, he cleared his throat.

"Do you know if the slaves will be gathering later tonight?"

Although his voice was cordial, his question quickly brought Mamie back to the full implication of the situation. He was indeed a slave buyer but apparently new at it. Mamie grunted to herself as she realized his pleasant manners would only last until he knew the 'rules' and 'language' of slave buying.

Feeling her daughter beginning to tremble again, Mamie knew she too understood why he was there.

"Naw s'ur," Mamie said, almost too quickly and thought for sure he would know she was lying.

"The slaves here don't mee' t'night," Mamie continued, staring down at the floor. "We's har'ly ever mee' enymo'." Aware of how fast she was still speaking, Mamie warned herself to slow down. "I's b'lieve yous mean Massa Thomas' slaves down the road a bit. Thay migh' be mee'in' t'night."

Mamie said no more as she silently prayed the stranger would go.

Noticing he wasn't saying anything, Mamie looked up at him. The look in his eyes told her he knew she had lied. Mamie's eyes quickly darted back to the floor as a very unsettling feeling ran through her stomach; a feeling that started her heart pounding rapidly and sweat rolling down her fore-head.

"Thank you, ma'am," the stranger said. Although his voice sounded regretful, there was no mistaking that he had said 'ma'am.' Surprised again by him referring to her as this, Mamie looked up in time to see him tip his hat. Their eyes met for a brief moment before Mamie hurriedly looked back down. Her eyes remained glued toward the floor until she heard him stepping away. She then hurriedly closed the door.

"Mama, wuz he a slave buyer?" Ruth asked. The sound of her voice saddened Mamie greatly. It just didn't seem right that a child so young had to live with the ever present fear of being taken and sold.

"I's b'lieves so child," Mamie said with a deep, dismal sigh of uncertainty. He just did not look, act, or sound like one of them. "Don't yous play near the open door enymo'," she continued. "Bad men like tha' one migh' see yous and take yous 'way." No sooner were the words out of her mouth than a strange feeling came to her heart.

Mamie quickly tried to push the feeling aside as she assured herself that the stranger was a new slave buyer and did not know how to act. He had not been taught that he wasn't to treat slaves like humans; he was not to say kind words, or smile, or remove or tip his hat. She assured herself that he would soon learn and once he had, he would be just as cruel and cold-hearted to them as all the rest who came to buy or admire Massa's 'animals'; a term one buyer had used when referring to them.

Mamie looked at her small, frail daughter who now stood trembling, looking helpless and frightened at her. She took the child in her arms and held her close, unable to bear the thought of this child being taken from her, too.

Though Mamie fought to keep her tears from falling, it was impossible. They rolled forth softly and steadily as she thought back to the time her nine year old son Daniel had been taken from her and sold. Closing her eyes she tried to control the tears that now caused her entire body to slightly tremble. The recollection of that day was still very painful.

Mamie felt her daughter's small arms squeeze her tighter as the child said, "It's gon' be all righ', mama." Mamie *knew* differently as she continued thinking back to the day Daniel was taken away and how she screamed and pleaded with Massa to keep him but to no avail. She had then turned to the Lord and asked him to somehow not let her son suffer; to let him feel her love no matter how hard the trials that came his way.

Later that same day, Mamie received the news that her son had been shot and killed as he tried to run away. The news of his death caused her heart to grieve terribly; nevertheless, she found some comfort in knowing that her son would never suffer loneliness or be in the hands of someone who might have brutally mistreated him. She was also comforted in knowing that he had had a chance to be with her for nine years and knew *who* she was.

Mamie never knew her mother; she had been taken as a baby and raised with several other babies by an older slave woman who had been too ill and too old to work Massa's fields. It was not until she had her son Daniel that she knew the good, happy feeling love could bring. She couldn't wait to come in from the fields each day to hold him. Every second she held him in her arms she told him over and over how much she loved him. She wanted him to *know* he had a mother who loved and wanted him since she also knew in her heart that the day would come when he would be taken and sold. When it finally happened, she had prayed he would always remember her love, and when news came of his death, she again prayed he had remembered he was loved.

When Mamie became pregnant with Ruth, she had vowed to herself that the child would never be taken from her. The slaves, though feeling it would never work, supported her in any way they could. On the night the baby was born, they told Massa it had been born dead. They then helped her plot and plan ways to hide and care for the child.

"Mama, it be all righ'. He be gon' now," Ruth said, breaking into her mother's thoughts. The child pulled gently away and stood looking pitifully at Mamie for a few seconds before gently wiping away her mother's tears.

"Guess who love yous, mama?" Ruth said in an effort to get her mother to smile.

"Yous do, baby girl," Mamie said as she pulled the child back into her arms. "And mama love yous, too."

Mamie tried to smile in spite of the deep fear and sorrow her heart was feeling. As she thought about how much she had gone through in losing her son and in trying to keep Ruth a secret, it was hard for her to feel peace and happiness

"He be gon' for good, righ' mama?" Ruth asked.

"Yes child, I's think so," her mother replied.

After a short while Mamie opened her door a small crack and peeked out to be certain. When she didn't see him, she told Ruth to stay inside and not let anyone in. Her words brought a look of fear into Ruth's eyes as the child grabbed her mother's arm tightly. Mamie assured her she would be right back.

"I's need to warn the others and make sho' we don't gather t'night." Mamie told her. "Tha' bad man be gon' and yous have nothin' a'tall to fear no mo', but there be others like him. It jus' be best we don't gather t'night." Mamie forced a smile and hugged Ruth firmly as she left and went from shack to shack telling the other slaves what had happened, expanding on the story as she went and making sure she looked and sounded terrified by the whole ordeal. However, though Mamie's voice, words, and appearance may have given the slaves that impression, her heart felt differently.

As the strange feeling persisted, Mamie sought headstrong to convince herself she was doing the right thing in warning the others. Nevertheless, her conscience fought her to the contrary. It reminded her of how courteous the stranger had been; how he had, unquestionably, treated her as a human being and not as a thing unworthy of his respect.

"But tha' be 'cause he be new at this." Mamie argued with her conscience as she turned to start for her shack. "When he learns, he be jus' as mean as the rest of them."

With that as her final argument, Mamie hurried to her shack. Once inside, she told Ruth they had to be very careful and not let the bad people see her. The child promised her she would be.

"I's don't want to lea'e yous, mama, e'er," Ruth said.

"Yous won't, child. Yous will *ne'er* lea'e yo' mama," Mamie assured her with the same determination she had had before the child was born.

Mamie's fear of losing Ruth gradually diminished as time passed. She had almost forgotten the stranger's visit until one morning while on their way to work a slave called Eli asked her if she knew that the overseer had been outside her shack during the early part of the night.

"He's look' like he sees a ghos'," old man Eli said.

Shaking her head no, Mamie jokingly turned to the other slaves and said, "Guess what ever'body? Ol' overseer mus' kno' I's be plannin' to run 'way, so which of yous tells him?"

They all started laughing as they pointed at each other. All of a sudden a feeling hit Mamie so hard that she gasped for air.

"Now Ms Mamie, don't yous start actin' crazy with us; we's kno' yous not crazy," someone said jokingly. Mamie did not respond but began looking around with tremendous suspicion on her face.

"Ms Mamie, what be wrong?" Old man Eli asked, his own face showing worry.

"Ol overseer, where he be?" Mamie questioned him. "Where he be?" She immediately repeated, a terrifying thought racing through her mind.

Before anyone could answer, Mamie took off running toward the shacks. Fear gripped tightly at her heart as her stomach got a very queasy feeling. She knew the overseer had indeed seen a ghost; a ghost that had been hidden from him and Massa for eight years.

"Pleas', dear Lord, pleas', not agin," Mamie prayed aloud repeatedly as she raced toward her shack. She also yelled at herself, wondering how she could have been so foolish as to believe the stranger wouldn't tell Massa about the child.

"Pleas', dear Lord, pleas' shield her from their sigh'; pleas' do this one merc'ful thang for me," she continued pleading as she ran as fast as her legs would carry her, her tears virtually blinding the path.

When Mamie came around the corner to the front of the shacks, the fear inside her became real as she saw the overseer push unsuccessfully on the door. For a brief moment she felt a sigh of relief; Ruth had apparently remembered to put the old wooden latch on the door. The small comfort quickly vanished as she watched in horror as the overseer raised a foot and gave the door one hard kick, causing it to practically fall off its hinges.

"Noooooooooo," Mamie screamed as she rushed forward to stop them. Neither reacted to her scream as they hurried inside. Upon reaching them, Mamie grabbed the back of Massa's shirt. He turned and glared at her with absolute surprise. His look scared Mamie so terribly until she barely saw his arm go up, but within seconds she felt the powerful blow to the side of her face. She screamed as she lost her balance and the side of her face crashed hard against the sharp, jagged edge of the dangling door. At that moment she heard Ruth scream, too.

For a brief moment Mamie thought the blow had caused her to lose her eyesight; everything was dark and spinning. Praying, she struggled to get back on her feet.

"Pleas' help me, dear Lord," she prayed. "Pleas' give me the streng'h to stand and do what I's can fo' my child." As Mamie prayed, she heard the repeated screams of her child: "Mama, help me. Pleas' mama, pleas' pleas, help me."

Somehow Mamie found the strength to get back on her feet. She rose, straight and tall, no longer aware of her pains, but those of her child. Even though things were still quite blurred, she could see them. The overseer was dragging her child from where she was tucked within the old straw bed. Massa was a couple of feet in front of Mamie watching as the child screamed and struggled to free herself. Mamie charged forward, nearly knocking him over as she tore into the overseer. Grabbing his arm she bit down hard into his flesh, determined not let go of it until he let go of her child. He let out a blood-curdling scream just as something solid and hard concurrently hit Mamie squarely in the back. The blow broke her grip on the overseer's arm but at the same time enraged her more.

Mamie's failure to fall from the blow surprised Massa, for when she turned on him, looking and sounding like a mad woman, his eyes grew large with panic. He made a dash for the door, tripped and almost fell as he did so. Mamie had barely started after him when a sharp pain to the back of her head sent her crashing headlong into an old table, the top of her left eye hitting the corner of it. For a moment everything went dark before Mamie rolled over in time to see the overseer grab Ruth and hurry out the door.

"Yous let go of my child," Mamie cried out weakly, dragging herself as fast as she could toward the door. "Let go of *my* child," she repeated upon reaching the outside. Massa, looking fully in control, sat on his horse holding a gun.

"This can't be *your* child," he said as Mamie struggled to remain conscience. "Your child *died*, remember?" His voice, sounding extremely vindictive, matched the look on his face. "*This* apparently is a runaway. And since I have taken care of it all these years, it's about time I sold it."

"Pleas', pleas' Massa, s'ur, don't take my child," Mamie pleaded as blood dripped down her face. "She be all I's got. Pleas', *pleas'* s'ur, don't take her."

"Mama," Ruth moaned sadly as she reached a tiny hand toward her mother, but before Mamie could say anything, they hurriedly rode away.

"Pleas' don't take her 'way," Mamie cried as she pounded her fist against the old porch.

"Ms Mamie don't." Mamie heard old man Eli say as he placed a hand gently on her shoulder. "Pleas' don't; thay will kill yous *and* yo' child," he said.

Mamie looked up to see tears in his eyes as he stared down the road where only a trail of dust was still visible.

"I's want my child, Eli. Thay take her but she be mine. *She be mine*," Mamie sobbed as she held his arm tightly.

"No, Ms Mamie, she not be yo' child. She b'longs to Massa on this here earth. Yous b'long to Massa, too; we's all b'long to him and there ain't nothin' yous kan do 'bout that; *nothin' at all*," he said as he stared at her. "Massa's got the righ' to take that child and eny other child here. Yous kno' that. Now yous stop actin' all crazy, and lets take care of that nas'y cut on yo' face and eye."

Mamie pushed his hands off her and stared coldly into his eyes. "Yous let me be. *Let me be*," she shouted at him.

Old man Eli turned and slowly limped away. Mamie continued sitting there crying, rocking back and forth as she stared down the empty dirt road. A very haunting thought kept going through Mamie's mind—had she caused them to take the child? She thought about how it appeared that Ruth had securely hidden herself among the straws in the old bed as she'd been taught. Would they have found her if she had not reacted to her mother's scream. The thought of her mistake added greatly to the grief of her heart.

Late into the evening she remained there crying and asking the good Lord why; why wasn't there any happiness in this world for her.

Once, as Mamie finished talking aloud to the Lord, a streak of lightning illuminated the sky, bringing back memories of the many times she had sat by an old tree crying for a mammy to love her. Back then the lightning's bright, beautiful colors always made her smile, but there was no magic in it for her now, especially not tonight. There was only the never ending reminder of the pains and heartaches of slavery; the anguish of having no rights, not even to your own children.

As the sky grew darker and the hour late, different slaves tried to get her to go inside, but Mamie ignored them and their pleas. Many spoke with concern about her swollen eye and the long, open gash on the side of her face. Mamie was well aware of how swollen her eye had become as well as the horrendous pains in her stomach and back, but there was not one bodily affliction that could equal the pains Mamie's heart was feeling.

The night finally brought an end to movement outside and inside the slaves' shacks. Mamie looked back at her shack, all dark and quiet. She dreaded the thought of having to ever go inside it again; dreaded the thought of being alone and lonely; dreaded never hearing her child playing quietly off to the side of the room; and dreaded the familiar agony her heart would feel with each coming day.

Not wanting to go inside, Mamie turned her thoughts back to all that had happened that day. She felt a small amount of comfort in knowing she had, for once in her life, stood up and fought for something she wanted; She had been willing to die if dying meant saving her child. She also realized that her lack of fear had given her the courage to stand up and fight; courage that enabled her to feel no fear of Massa or the overseer. Mamie also knew it would be a day Massa would not forget and neither would she, but they would remember it for completely different reasons.

Mamie's tears continued to fall even though she knew in her heart that her crying was in vain. She finally decided she might as well go inside as she faced reality—she was a slave, a nobody..

As if he had heard Mamie's thinking, old man Eli came out and asked her if she was okay.

"Kan yous help me to my shack, Eli?" Mamie asked and was surprised at the calm of her own voice.

"I's will, Ms Mamie. Yous need to take care of tha' eye 'fo' yous lose all sigh' in it. It be lookin' migh'y ter'ble."

Struggling together, Eli managed to get Mamie up far enough to have her lean against him as he slowly hobbled to her shack. Once inside he told Mamie to rest while he tried to put something together to help her eye.

Mamie then heard Eli catch his breath as if something had startled him.

"Who be you, s'ur?" Mamie heard him say. She turned her head to see who he was talking to but saw no one.

"Eli, who yous be talkin' to?" Mamie asked as she saw him moving toward the opened door. Mamie then heard old man Eli's voice and that of another man. They both spoke so low that she could not make out what was being said. After the exchange of a few more words, Mamie heard old man Eli say, "Thank yous kindly, s'ur, and pleas' thank the good Lord too for sendin' yous."

Whenever old man Eli was given something, he would always thank the person and then tell the person to thank the good Lord even though he always thanked the good Lord himself. Mamie could also tell from old man Eli saying 's'ur' that the person was white. They *had* to say 'sir' when talking to Massa or any other white man.

"Who be it Eli?" Mamie asked before Eli could step back inside and close the door. When he turned toward her, he looked as if he had seen a ghost.

"It be a white man, Ms Mamie. Not Massa or the overseer, but some other tall white man. He brough' this here jar of stuff for yo' bruis's." He held up a small jar.

"A white man?" Mamie asked, shocked that Massa would have someone bring something to help her. "Why Massa do's tha'?"

"I's don't think he be fro' Massa. Naw, this man spoke dif'ent, Ms Mamie. Sum'un warm 'bout that man and his voice. I's don't think Massa kno' he be here."

Mamie didn't want to disagree with old man Eli; didn't want him to think she was trying to 'back talk' him, even though she felt Massa had sent the man. Mamie had to admit though that it was something Massa had never done before.

Old man Eli cleaned the open cut on the side of Mamie's face the best he could. He tried to wash her eye, but she cried out in pain at his mere touch on it. He feared mightily that she would lose the use of it, but said for her to put her trust in the good Lord to save it.

He finally said he had best be going. Mamie thanked him and watched him move hesitantly toward the door. He stopped just as he got to it and turned to her with a strange look on his face.

"I's tell yous, Ms Mamie, tha' white man sho' be dif'ent," he said, so quietly that Mamie wasn't sure if he was talking to her or himself.

Mamie didn't give any thought to what old man Eli said about the white man. After she finished rubbing some of the liquid from the jar on as much of her back as she could, she gently touched her eye. Feeling the huge lump on it, Mamie prayed and asked the good Lord to please not let her lose her sight. "These ol' eyes be all I's got to help me someday find my child," Mamie whispered quietly.

After praying Mamie sighed heavily with hopelessness and tried to go to sleep, but couldn't. Upon closing her eyes she saw her child; her tiny hand reaching out to her as she lay helplessly across that horse. She could still clearly hear her saying, "Mama, pleas' help me." Mamie's tears started flowing again.

Mamie was unable to stand or see very well the next day. She expected Massa to make her go to the fields anyway, but he didn't. She almost felt she sensed some sympathy in him when he saw her condition the next day and told her she'd better not go to work for a while. He turned away and left before she could say, "thank you, s'ur."

True to his word, Massa didn't have her go back to the fields the next day nor the day after, but during that time, neither did she rest. The empty and lonely feeling in her shack made it impossible for her grief-stricken heart and mind to rest.

By the third morning, however, Mamie realized she had finally fallen asleep when she opened her eyes to see the morning sun shining through the cracks. She lay there wondering if Massa would soon have her return to the fields even though she was still in no condition to work. She nevertheless accepted the fact that she would have to return to work. She felt a small second of gratitude to Massa for what rest he had allowed her to have, though the hatred she felt toward him for taking her child far outweighed the gratitude.

Thoughts of Mamie's child always came rushing back, as did the guilt, causing her heart to feel heavy with grief, especially when she thought about her promise to the child to never let her be taken; a promise that was foolish of any slave to make.

"Pleas' fo'give me child," Mamie muttered quietly. "I's did try."

A knock at the door one morning immediately brought fear to Mamie's heart. She felt certain it was Massa or the overseer coming to to tell her to get to the fields with the other slaves. She then realized she was being silly thinking it was the overseer or anyone white; they never knocked on a slave's door.

"Who be there?" Mamie asked weakly.

The door opened slowly, and a slave entered. He didn't look like any of the slaves on Massa's place; Mamie knew most of them. He looked at her; actually, he stared at her eye as she stared at him.

"Yous' sho' do look pit'ful with that fat thang ove' yo' eye. Is yo' eye still un'er there?" He finally asked, looking as if he was afraid to move from the door.

"I's don't kno'." Mamie answered him earnestly.

"Well it sho's make yous look ugly," he said just as earnestly.

"Who yous be, and what yous want?" Mamie asked him again.

"Well, I's tells yous why I's here if yous be the righ' one to tell," he said rather nervously as he remained by the door.

"What yous mean, *if* I's be the righ' one to tell. To tell *what?*" Mamie demanded, her voice beginning to tremble with fear as the thought entered her mind that maybe he had come to tell her something awful had happened to her child.

"Yous had a girl child that be took to town to be sold?" He asked.

"Oh Lord, no," Mamie moaned. "Pleas' don't tell me my girl be dead, too." She rolled out of bed, crying loudly.

"I's not tells yous yo' child be dead," he said, raising his voice to make her hear him. "I's jus' comes to tell yous where yo' child be."

"My child, yous kno' 'bout my child. Where she be? Is she all right? Pleas', pleas' tell me." Mamie spoke so quickly that he had no time to answer. As she started toward him, he backed against the door, his eyes large with fright as he stared at her swollen eye. Mamie stopped.

"Pleas', tells me my child be all righ'," Mamie said pleadingly.

"I's don't kno' if yo' child be okay. I's only kno' that she gon' be sold in town in the morn'," he said as he opened the door and ran.

Mamie called out to him as she moved to the door as fast as she could, but by the time she got there, he was no where to be seen. She stood in the opened doorway thinking about what he had said and wondered who had sent him to tell her. All of a sudden, the who and why didn't matter, only seeing her child again. Mamie knew she had to go see her even though she knew Massa would have her beaten unmercifully.

Knowing she had to wait until dark before starting her journey, Mamie returned to her bed to rest. As she lay there, her heart felt no fear; she relished in the thought of seeing her baby one more time. Mamie also knew that seeing her would be all she could do, but that in itself would be enough.

Old man Eli came to bring Mamie a bite to eat when the slaves came in from the fields as he had for the past few days. He checked her eye and shook his head.

"I's fear yous migh' lose tha' eye," he said sadly.

"I's don't think I's will. I's be able to see a peep of ligh' with it alrea'y," Mamie lied. She just couldn't bear the thought of not having her full sight. She told him the stuff Massa had sent for her bruises had helped a lot and she had felt few pains all day.

"Massa didn't send no man," old man Eli said rather adamantly. "It be some kind stranger."

Mamie didn't say anything else on the matter. She could see that old man Eli was determined to believe the help had not come from Massa. They both remained quiet for quite awhile. Mamie finally broke the silence. Knowing old man Eli had once tried to run away from Massa when he was first

taken from his mammy, she decided to see what he would say
when she told him she was going to go see her child.

"Eli, when yous ran 'way to find yo' mammy, if yous kno'
thay gon' cut off yo' foot, would yous still have gon'?"

"Yes, Ms Mamie, I's sho' would have. I's be not scare'.
I's love' my mammy and all I's want wuz to see and be with
her agin. I's wuz willin' to die and go home to the good Lord
if I's had to."

"I's want to see my child agin," Mamie said, hoping he
would advise her to try.

"Well, Ms Mamie, yous best put tha' child in the Lord's
hand and go on. Yous kno' she be gon' and all yo' thinkin'
'bout seein' her ain't gon' help a thang. Yous migh' as well
go on and be as happy as yous kan be in this world."

Mamie didn't say any more and neither did old man Eli.
After making sure she had water he left. A part of her wanted
to tell him what she was going to do, a part of her didn't, and
still another part of her felt he already knew.

Mamie waited until the sky turned slightly dark and then
gathered the few things she was taking: a bottle of water, the
piece of bread old man Eli had brought her, and the small jar
of medicine. She said a prayer, asking the good Lord to guide

her path and keep a protective arm around her. As she rose from praying, she felt complete calmness.

Mamie didn't have any problem sneaking out of her shack without any of the slaves seeing her; they were gathered at old man Eli's shack for a prayer meeting. As she eased past the shacks, she heard old man Eli praying for her, asking the good Lord to help her body and mind to heal from the pains they were going through. She paused for a few seconds to listen to more of his words and then started on her way.

Mamie walked and ran as best she could toward the direction she thought town to be. It was not an easy journey. Several times she feared she had lost her way. The darkness, coupled with unfamiliar surroundings, frightened her. Each time Mamie felt lost and afraid, she would stop and pray real hard for the good Lord to help her. Lightning would soon follow her prayer, giving light to a path before her.

As Mamie stumbled on through the night, thoughts of a time when a slave had run away came to her mind. The slave had announced to them the next morning that he had run away. They had all stopped and looked at him questionably.

"I's runs 'way las' nigh'," he repeated.

Silence again followed as they all stared at him. Finally someone said, "So fool if yous runs 'way las' nigh' why yous still here now?"

The slave who had announced that he'd run away looked at the one who had asked the question as if he could not believe he didn't know why. "Cause," he said with indignation. "Cause this here fool runs and runs but all my runun' brin's me righ' back to here, that's why I's be here now!"

Mamie found herself smiling now as she asked the Lord to please not let the same thing happen to her; she didn't want to be going in circles.

There were times when she wanted to rest but wouldn't. Instead, she prayed that the Lord would continue to comfort and strengthen her weary soul.

When daylight finally appeared across the sky, Mamie's eyes beheld the town in a short distance. Smiling with joy, she uttered a quiet, heartfelt 'thank you' to the Lord as she looked down, and then, with disbelief, gently reached down and touched her tireless feet.

Mamie walked until she found the auction block. She located some barrels nearby and sat down behind one. While she waited for the slaves to be brought out, she listened as the town's people started to gather near the block. They were laughing and talking with pleasure as if at a party. Neither their laughter nor conversations revealed any concern that they were there to purchase human beings. A wretched feeling filled Mamie's heart, and she shook her head sadly. She wondered if they had ever had a child or loved one torn from their bosom and sold.

A hush soon fell upon the crowd. Mamie knew the slaves must be going up on the auction block by the "Aaaahh" from the crowd. She stood for the first time since she had arrived and was surprised to see how many people had gathered. Looking at them, Mamie was deeply disheartened by the approving smiles they had on their faces as they stared at the line of slaves on the block.

The crowd's reaction pleased the auctioneer. He beamed with pride as he gave the crowd a friendly and cheerful nod. Mamie moved her attention from him to the slaves standing on the block. Their faces showed the sadness and fear their hearts surely felt.

Mamie searched the line frantically for Ruth. Amidst the noise of the crowd she could hear the soft crying of someone and knew it was her child. She then realized it was Ruth that the auctioneer now stood before and was saying something to. Ruth wiped continually at her eyes, seemingly trying to stop her tears from falling but unable to do so.

Still laughing and talking to each other as they pointed to different slaves, the people began moving closer toward the auction block. Some of the women had a hand over their nose, frowning as if there was a very unpleasant smell. None seemed aware of the sad looks on the faces of the slaves, especially the children. Mamie looked around again at the crowd and then at the slaves waiting to be sold. It was a very pitiful sight, both that of the buyers and those to be bought. Mamie wanted to yell out to them that they had feeling; that they were human beings, too. Instead, something inside told her to *pray*.

Trying to control her anger, Mamie stared down at the ground for a brief moment and wondered what to pray for. She knew praying would not enable her to have her child back. She gasped when the thought came that she should pray for them; not the slaves, but for the people she was sur-rounded by. The thought of praying for them angered Mamie. She could in no way pray for the people who stood saying such awful things. She told the Lord she had no words of prayer for 'them,' but she did for those who were being sold—her own child being one of them. But the feeling came again, warm but firm, for whom she was to pray. This time she obeyed.

After praying for 'them,' Mamie asked the Lord to please grant her one thing.

"Since yous kant 'liver my child back to me, pleas' let her go to someone with a kind heart. I's not only askin' this for me but for my child, too." Mamie silently pleaded.

Mamie looked at her child, hoping she would somehow see her. The auctioneer was still saying something to her and whatever he was saying made Ruth sob even harder. His voice then rose above the noise of the crowd as he yelled at her to stop her crying. Ruth tried. Mamie could see that she was really trying hard to stop but couldn't. A little slave boy of five or six standing next to her, reached over and took her hand in his small little hand, saying something to her as he did. Ruth still could not stop crying. He then stood patting her on her shoulder. Mamie's eyes clouded with tears and her heart swelled with pride and gratitude as she observed the young boy and the comfort he sought to give her child.

As the crowd quieted down, Mamie again heard the auctioneer warn Ruth to stop crying; there was no mistaking the anger and viciousness of his voice. Mamie started praying to the good Lord to please help Ruth to stop crying, but she watched in horror and pain as the auctioneer hit the child across the back of her head with an object he had in his hand. Ruth lost her balance from the blow and fell, face first, onto the wooden board where she was standing.

The child lay there screaming as the auctioneer yelled at her to shut up and get back on her feet. The same little slave boy who had reached over to comfort her, now stooped down and pulled at Ruth to get up, his own tears very visible. With his help, she finally managed to do so. As she did, Mamie could see blood pouring from her nose. It also looked as if the edge of the board had made a gash on her lower lip. Ruth's eyes appeared frightened as she cried uncontrollably. Her tiny hands went up to her face as she tried to catch the flowing blood. The little boy ripped off a piece of his already torn shirt and handed it to her.

Mamie could stand no more! She had barely started forward when someone grabbed her arm. Ready to yell at whoever it was to let go of her, Mamie looked into the eyes of a tall, white man. She expected to see anger and hear cruel words, but instead, the eyes staring back at her looked deeply sad and the words he spoke supported the feeling she saw .

"Please don't," he said pleadingly. "You will only make matters worse for the child. Please don't cause greater suffering to her."

"But that be *my* child," Mamie said weakly, her strength of will weakening as her eyes filled with tears. He nodded a look of understanding.

"I will see what I can do," he acknowledged as he let go of her arm.

Mamie watched as he made his way through the crowd. As she watched him she felt a sense of hope. She also felt she had seen those eyes and heard that voice before.

The man made his way up to where the slaves stood and over to Mamie's child. A hush fell upon the crowd as all eyes were on him. Gently he leaned the child's head back a little as he reached into his pocket and took out a handkerchief. Instead of handing it to her, he knelt before her and began wiping at the blood that was steadily flowing down her face. The crowd gasped in horror as someone said, "How can he!"

The tall man was saying something to the child. Since the crowd stood watching silently in shock, his words, warm and sincere, flowed clearly for all to hear.

"Be strong and have courage, child. The Lord is with you and will comfort you," he said.

Ruth had been trembling greatly but seemed to grow calm as she stared at the man with tear-filled eyes. He gave her a gentle pat on the arm and said, "Fear not." He then began wiping away her tears with his fingers. The crowd, upon seeing this, went wild. They began yelling cruel, ugly things at him. Someone even threw a dark, heavy looking object that hit him in the back, but he never reacted to their words nor the pain the object surely must have caused. He stood calmly helping the child until he must have felt certain she was all right.

When he finally started walking away, a chant broke out to "get him, get him," but no one rushed forward to do so. Mamie looked at her child and somehow the child's eyes found hers among the crowd. Mamie smiled. Ruth was no longer crying, although her face looked extremely sad as she smiled, too. She then reached down and touched her ankle. Mamie saw why, and her heart cried warmly with tears of love. Her child had touched the old wood chip that was tied around her ankle. Mamie had given one to both Ruth and Daniel when they each turned two. She had put it around their ankle so they would know she was thinking about them when she was off in the fields working all day. She had told each of them how it was an "I love you" wood chip, and when touched, they would feel her love. She also wore one around her ankle.

Mamie knelt down and touched hers, too. They both smiled in spite of the sadness and grief their hearts were feeling. With her lips moving painfully slow, Ruth silently began mouthing the words to one of the songs they often sang.

> Didn't my Lord deliver Daniel,
> Deliver Daniel, deliver Daniel?
> Didn't my Lord deliver Daniel
> Then why not every man?
>
> He delivered Daniel from the lion's den
> Jonah from the belly of the whale
> The Hebrew children from the fiery furnace,
> Then why not *me*?

Smiling and crying, Mamie began mouthing the words with her. As Mamie did she wanted so very much to just be able to go hold her child in her arms one last time but knew she couldn't.

Over and over they silently mouthed the words of that song until Ruth was sold. When she was bought, they both looked at each other one last time as their tears began falling more steadily. Ruth raised her tiny hand and waved bye. They each then leaned over and once again touched their wood chip. The little slave boy standing next to Ruth, reached out and gave her a hug, his face looking both happy and sad. He watched her as she was being led off the block and then lowered his head, but not before Mamie saw tears rolling down his face. Seeing his tears, Mamie prayed to the good Lord to comfort him and to bless him to go to someone kind.

Turning her attention back to Ruth, Mamie tried to see who had bought her but couldn't. She caught a glimpse of a young couple's back as her child followed them to a wagon. A man rushed forward with some chains to chain Ruth and the other slaves on the wagon, but the couple shook their head no. Mamie watched as Ruth sat next to an older woman.

The couple stood talking for a few seconds and then the man rushed back toward the auction block. Ruth sat with her head down and her hands over her face. From the way her body was shaking, Mamie knew she was sobbing. The older woman put her arm around her; her own tears very noticeable.

The man soon returned and with him was the small slave boy. He climbed upon the wagon and walked over and tapped Ruth on the head. Ruth looked up, and seeing him, jumped up and hugged him. He sat down by her with a big smile on his face. Their happiness in being together touched Mamie deeply. She knew that little boy would somehow watch over Ruth. She then thanked the good Lord for him and the older woman.

Although her child could no longer see her, Mamie stood, with tears rolling down her face, waving bye and mouthing the words to the song long after the wagon was out of sight. She then turned to begin the long, lonely walk back to Massa's place. As she turned to leave, she felt a gentle tug on her arm. She turned to see a young white lady with dark hair staring at her with tears in her eyes, too.

"Please," she said as she handed Mamie a small bag, squeezed her hand gently, then turned and hurried away.

Puzzled, Mamie slowly opened the bag and immediately stared in the direction the lady had gone.

"Thank yous, ma'am," Mamie murmured softly as she again turned to begin her long, lonely journey home.

I had not power to ask his name,
Whereto he went, or whence he came

Chapter Two

God's Friend

It was late night by the time Mamie got back to the shacks. Old man Eli was the only slave not inside and asleep. He sat on his old broken-down porch holding something in his hands. Upon seeing her, he quickly got up, hobbled over, and gave her a hug.

"Ms Mamie, I's' be worry sick 'bout yous. I's been prayin' migh'ly yous be okay. I's so happy yous back. Yous mus' be migh'y hun'ry."

"No Eli, I's be migh'y full, migh'y full."

"Did yous see yo' child."

"How yous kno' tha' be wha' I's be gon' to do?" Mamie asked him, pleased that he had known.

"Oh, Ms Mamie, I's could tell by yo' voice when yous asks me 'bout runnin' 'way to find my mammy. So, did yous see her?" he asked, smiling as if he already knew the answer.

Mamie nodded yes and broke into tears.

"Yous says yes, yous smilin', but yous also cryin'. What hap'en' Ms Mamie?" He asked, looking confused and deeply concerned.

Mamie then told him all that had happened in town; about the people, her child crying, the little slave boy, and the two kind white strangers who had helped. She was about to tell him about the couple who bought her child and the little boy, but old man Eli interrupted her.

"Ms Mamie, wha' did tha' white man look like?" He asked as if he might know him.

Mamie assured him it had not been Massa or the overseer. She was about to continue when he interrupted her again.

"Ms Mamie, I's kno' it not be one of thim. Pleas', tell me, wha' did he look and soun' like?" Old man Eli not only looked very serious, but his words gave her a feeling he really thought he knew the man.

It was not until Mamie started describing to old man Eli what the man looked like that she remembered why the man had looked familiar; he was the same one who had come inquiring whether the slaves would be meeting. The realization of who he was caused her to stop in the middle of a sentence. Old man Eli asked what was wrong. She shook her head to indicate nothing.

"Ms Mamie, yous sho' don't look like nothin's wrong; yous look real scare'," he said.

"Not scare', Eli. Jus' real 'fused righ' now," Mamie said as many questions began flooding her heart concerning the strange white man.

Mamie didn't realize she was shaking her head until old man Eli grabbed her arm and asked what was wrong. She lied and said she was grief-stricken. She then changed the subject and asked if Massa or the overseer had asked about her.

"Tha' ol' overseer ask' 'bout yous, Ms Mamie, and when he learns yous be gon' he rush' 'way to Massa's house to tell him. I's don't kno' wha' Massa says to him, but he comes back lookin' all mad. He be real quiet, jus' kept lookin' at us as if warnin' us we bet'er not git no kind of no'ion to do nothin crazy. 'Nough 'bout Massa and ol' overseer, how's tha' eye of yo's?"

Mamie lied and told him it was doing mighty fine. The truth being the sight from it was quite poor. She feared greatly that she would never be able to see clearly again, but didn't have the heart to tell old man Eli or any of the other slaves.

Old man Eli then asked her again about the white man who had helped her child; he seemed most curious about him. Mamie lied and told him she was mighty tired and would tell him about the man some other time.

"I's un'erstands," old man Eli said. Mamie started to stand, but he asked her to wait a moment.

"I's got one mo' thang I's want to say to yous Ms Mamie 'fo' yous go."

He stared down at the object in his hands. "I's don't kno' how much lon'er the good Lord gon' let me be 'round, but if my time be t'mor'ow or years fro' now, I's still like to give this to yous now." He held the object out toward Mamie. It was not until her hand touched it did she realize what it was— his Bible; the *only* book any of them had ever seen. It was greatly worn, but still one they all admired and was proud to see old man Eli with.

"Eli," Mamie said most solemnly. "I's kant have this."

"Yes yous kan, Ms Mamie."

Mamie opened it and closed it quickly. She looked at Eli with a frightened look in her eyes.

"Oh Eli, the good Lord kno' I's kant have this. I's kant read."

"Shuss," he said putting a finger to his lip. "With the good Lord, all thangs be pos'ble. Now yous keep this here book even if yous think yous kant read."

Mamie had never been given a gift before, and her tears began to fall. She was overwhelmed by the thoughtfulness of this old man and saddened that her first gift was one she could not even use. She thanked him wholeheartedly; promised him she would take care of it, but again asked him if he was sure he wanted her to have it. He nodded his head.

"But I's kno' this book means a lot to yous," Mamie said.

"Ms Mamie, I's will carry to my grave the words of the good Lord in here," he touched his heart. "I's want yous to keep it here on the good Lord's earth and share it with others so that thay someday migh' be able to do the same. It be the only thang I's own to leave b'hind, Ms Mamie. Now yous go on to yo' shack and git some' res'; mornin' gon' come awful soon."

Mamie thanked him again and walked slowly toward her shack with it clutched tightly against her heart. When she got there she found the door securely back on its hinges. Inside she looked slowly around and tried not to think about how quiet and lonely the place felt, but couldn't. She missed her child terribly and longed to have her come put her hands over her eyes and say, "Guess who loves yous mama, and you's will guess who I's be."

Grief stricken, Mamie sat down on her old chair and remained there until the morning light seeped through. Not wanting to, she slowly got up and prepared to face life without ever being able to come home to her child again.

The overseer stared at Mamie as she joined the other slaves to go to the fields, but he did not say anything. Once in the field, he instructed the slave child carrying water not to give any to her the entire day. She didn't say a word. She quietly continued with her work although the hot sun and work made her mighty thirsty. She sought to forget her thirst by turning her thoughts to those last moments of seeing her child. Those moments enabled her to endure that day and the coming ones as the punishment of not being given water continued for three more days. It was still a small price to pay.

Old man Eli refused to have water, too. He said he could not drink knowing that she had to go without. Mamie pleaded with him to drink, especially since his health hadn't been good lately, but no matter how hard she tried to tell him not to thirst because of her, he still continued to.

During the days Mamie had to go without water, her thoughts often went back to the two strangers who had helped her, especially the tall white man who had helped her child. She kept seeing him in her mind and his acts of kindness. Deep within her heart she felt certain he had to be a man of God, a good man of God. Although she reminded herself that she had known other men who claimed to be men of God, but they were more like men of the devil. They encouraged the owners to beat the slaves and make sure they understood who were their masters.

"For it is the will of God that they obey you; they must always know that you are indeed their *master*," they would preach with great conviction to the slave owners. Yet, in comparing those supposedly 'good' men of God to the tall, white man, she knew there was a significant difference.

One morning as they were in the field, the overseer counted them and realized one was missing. He asked who it was but none of them answered. They kept their heads down and worked as if they had not heard his question.

"Don't you dare ignore me," he yelled angrily.

"It be old man Eli," someone quickly said.

The overseer turned to the slave who had spoken. The slave stood looking down, his whole body trembling.

"Where is he?" The overseer asked him in a very nasty tone as he stared coldly at the slave.

"S'ur he be sick; he be *real* sick," the slave said, his voice shaking.

"*Sick*," yelled the overseer in the slave's face. "What do you mean, he's sick. Did *I* tell him to stay in his shack and be sick."

"Naw s'ur, yous didn't, but he be real..."

"I don't care how sick he is," he said, and then he looked at Mamie. "I tell you when you can or cannot do something," he said angrily. He mounted his horse and hurriedly rode toward the shacks.

Mamie feared for old man Eli. He was weak, too weak to get out of bed or he would have been in the fields no matter how sick he was. She prayed that once the overseer saw how sick and weak he was, he'd get some kind of help, but she soon realized she should have known that would never happen. Minutes later the overseer came riding just as hurriedly back. Mamie moaned aloud with sorrow as her eyes beheld the condition of poor old man Eli.

The overseer ordered two slaves, Thomas and Sam, to take Eli to the swamps and dump him. Mamie gasped, knowing that if old man Eli wasn't dead, he soon would be. The swamps were the worst kind of punishment for disobedience; not only would he be given no food or water, but he would also have to contend with the heat and flies.

At first the two didn't move, perhaps because they were feeling sorry for old man Eli, but the overseer yelled his orders again and they rushed to do it. When they picked old man Eli up, Mamie cried out and turned her head from the pitiful sight of his body. Old man Eli did not make a sound as the two lifted him off the ground. She asked the good Lord to please be merciful and let death come quickly if he was not dead before they got to the swamps with him. She knew that the flies and other insects at the swamps would greatly increase his suffering.

The swamps lay quite a ways off beyond some trees, but Thomas and Sam were gone much longer than it would ordinarily take someone to go there and come back. The overseer started acting a bit nervous as time passed and there was no sign of them. He kept looking anxiously toward the swamps as he led his horse slowly around the fields. Mamie, too, kept staring in the direction of the swamp but for a different reason.

She finally did see Sam and Thomas coming about the same time the overseer did. He started to ride toward them but stopped. As they got nearer, the expressions on their faces was very noticeable. They looked as if they had seen a ghost. The overseer immediately started asking them what had taken so long.

"I didn't tell you to bury him; I said to dump him," he yelled at them. They looked at each other as if surprised by what the overseer had just said.

"We's didn't, s'ur. That man bur..."

"I don't want to hear what you have to say," the overseer cut Sam off. "I have a good notion to beat both of you and drag you back to those swamps."

Thomas and Sam looked at each other again and then at the overseer. Their faces still had a bewildered look on them but neither showed fear at what the overseer had just said. Signs of fear were important if you didn't want to get beaten; they assured the overseer he was still in control.

"Don't stand there and look at me. Get that dumb look off your face and get to work." Both slaves slowly turned and

began working, but Mamie also noticed how both kept looking back at the overseer and then toward the swamps.

For the rest of the day Mamie kept eying those two. She
could tell that something was definitely different as they continued to sneak frequent looks toward the swamps. When
time came to get a drink of water, Mamie made her way over
to Sam.

"What happen' over there?" She whispered to him. He
turned quickly and looked nervously at her. He shook his
head, but his eyes told her differently.

"Don't yous lie to me," Mamie said sternly. "I's kno'
sum'un' did." She then walked to the water bucket for a
drink. When she turned to leave, Sam stood looking wide-
eyed at her.

It seemed to take forever for the work day to end. When
it did, Mamie quickly rushed over to Sam as they all started
for their shack. She wanted desperately to know what had
happened at the swamps.

"Sum'un' happen' at tha' swamp, and I's want to kno'
righ' now," Mamie said anxiously.

"Kant righ' now, Ms Mamie. There be lots to tell and I's
don't think it be bes' to tell yous with the overseer followin'

us. He migh' think sum'un' bad; like we be talkin' 'bout run-nin' way or sum'un' like tha'. I's come tell yous t'night when he be not 'round." She nodded with understanding though her heart cried with desperation to know then.

When they got to the shacks and lined up to get a bite of food, Mamie was further surprised by the actions of those two, especially Sam. He clapped his hands loudly to quiet the slaves.

"I's 'spose y'all kno's tha' old man Eli died t'day. I's think we should all bow our heads and thank the good Lord for his bein' with us so long and that he be no longer sufferin' but be real happy' and at peace. He be might' good to all of us," he said, his voice fading out as he was overcome with emotion.

Mamie had been so concerned over what had happened at the swamps that she had not thought much about old man Eli being gone forever. When Sam said what he did, tears welled up in her eyes. She was indeed one of the many who had been shown much love and kindness by old man Eli. A gloomy feeling filled her heart as she lowered her head and closed her eyes while Sam gave a prayer. She had never heard Sam pray and this too was strange.

Things were pretty quiet and solemn after his prayer. Very few words were spoken as they got their food. Sam went and sat near a tree after getting his food, and Mamie joined him once she had hers.

"Ms Mamie, my heart be real full righ' now," he said calmly as his eyes filled with tears. "Me and Thomas comes talk to yous t'night and tell yous ever' thang. I's think old man Eli would want yous to kno'." Mamie nodded her head as they then ate without another word. Once he had finished, he stood and slowly walked away. No longer wanting the remainder of her food, Mamie gave it to the child nearest her and walked to her shack and waited.

Hours later when Mamie heard a light knock on her door, she jumped, happy to finally hear it. She rushed over and opened the door. Thomas and Sam greeted her warmly as they came inside. They seated themselves on the floor. Sam immediately began talking.

"Ms Mamie, sum'un very strange happen' t'day. I's don't think yous gon" b'lieve us. I's thinkin' 'bout it and I's still not sure if I's be righ' in my mind or what. We be..."

"We be at the swamps with old man Eli, Ms Mamie, and this here white man walk up," Thomas said calmly, interrupting Sam's sentence. "Scare us real bad when we look and he be standin' there." He paused and looked at Sam.

Sam began talking about old man Eli's condition. "We be feelin' real sorry for old man Eli cause he not be all the way dead, and he be lookin' righ' pit'ful layin' there on the ground. I's look at Thomas and we both be cryin' for wha' we's have to do." Sam shook his head sadly as sobs choked his words, leaving him unable to continue.

"Ms Mamie, old man Eli nose and ears be bleedin' real bad. Yous kno' he be sick for a long time?" Thomas asked as his eyes filled with tears as he stared at her. She nodded her head.

"I's want' to do sum'un for him, Ms Mamie. Old man Eli be so good to ever'one." He wiped at his tears and tried to go on but couldn't.

Sam took over the story, but he too had difficulty speaking about what had happened.

"We's be sorrowin' real bad as we lay old man Eli on the ground. I's says to Thomas, 'Maybe we kan drag 'nough lea'es and co'er him from all the flies and thangs.' Thomas 'grees with me, and we wuz 'bout to start gittin' lea'es when we hears this here noise, like someone walkin' on those lea'es. We git might' scare' it be ol' overseer, and he gon' beat us for not dumpin' old man Eli and gittin' righ' back. We both look 'round and there stan's this here tall, white man. I's sees it not be ol' overseer but 'fraid it be a slave stea'er. He stan's lookin' at us, and we's stan's lookin' at him. I's jus' didn't kno' if we's should run or wha', Ms Mamie."

"The mo' we looks at each o'her, the mo' I's not sho'. I's be scare'." Thomas spoke up. "I's want' to run, but it seems tha' ol' ground jus' hold me there. I's even try'en' to stop lookin' that man in the eyes since white folks don't like us lookin' at them in thay eyes. But, Ms Mamie, even his eyes won't let me look 'way. He then walks 'ward us and my ol' heart real'y gets beatin' fast. I's didn't feel scare though, did yous Sam?" Thomas said all in one breathe.

Sam, very much caught up in what Thomas was saying, shook his head. "Sum'un 'bout his eyes won't let me be scare," he said.

"He walks close to us," Thomas continued. "And looks at old man Eli layin' there on that ground and then he looks back at us and asks if we's jus' gon' to lea'e Eli there like tha'. I's real'y look at him then, Ms Mamie, 'cause his voice be so kind. I's kno' then why I's not be 'fraid when lookin' in his eyes. Thay be real kind lookin. His voice and eyes both be real kind and sad.

"'Yas s'ur,' I's tells him. 'The overseer tells us to brin' him here and lea'e him on the ground jus' like tha'.'" He then kneels down by old man Eli and looks at him for a long time. Then I's kant 'b'lieve my eyes, Ms Mamie, at wha' tha' man did next," Thomas said as he rushed on. "Tha' man takes old man Eli's head and lif' it real slow from the ground and let it rest on his arm. I's hold my breath real hard when I's sees this 'cause his shirt be all white and clean and blood be runnin' fro' old man Eli's ears and nose. Tha' man acts like he did't sees none of tha' blood. He then takes this water thang off his shoulder and puts it to old man Eli's mouth." Thomas inhaled deeply, as if he was still in shock at what he had seen the man do. He shook his head and look at Mamie with disbelief in his eyes. "I's be tellin' you the tru'h, Ms Mamie. I's saw tha' white man let old man Eli drink out of his wa'er kan. Old man Eli could not drink fast, so tha' there white man gives him lit'le drops at a time."

"I's saw all this too, Ms Mamie," Sam said. "I's watch all tha' be gon' on, and I's kant b'lieve it ei'her. I's hear the man says to old man Eli 'Suffa no mo', the day com'th when you be crown with much glo'y.' I's not kno' what he means."

"Old man Eli had not open' his eyes or done nothin' all this time," Thomas said. "But Ms Mamie, when this man said those words to him, he open' his eyes and look' up at tha' white man. He then brough' one of his blood' hands up and touch tha' man's face and says sum'un' real strange to tha' man; he says, 'it be yous.'"

"Old man Eli then slo'ly close' his eyes, and he be gon'," Sam said, picking up the story.

"Why yous thinks old man Eli said 'it be yous' to him, Ms Mamie? Yous think he kno' tha' man?" Thomas asked.

Mamie shook her head as she wondered too what Eli had meant or why he would speak like he knew the man. It was then that she recalled the time someone had brought the small jar of medicine to old man Eli and his reaction afterwards, She felt certain it had to have been the kind, white stranger. Remembering how she had doubted old man Eli when he kept saying the man 'sho be dif'ent', Mamie moaned and shook her head.

"He sho' act like he did," Thomas said, and Mamie realized he thought she had been giving an answer to his question.

"I's sorry, Thomas," Mamie said. "I's was thinkin' about sum'un' old man Eli had said when I's shook my head. I's glad yous saw him lea'e this world with tha' stranger at his side showin' him love."

"Ms Mamie, I's be feelin' real good inside for old man Eli," Thomas said. "With all the pains he be havin,'" he smiles, "and look at peace 'fo' he dies."

One of them then told her how the white man let old man Eli lie for a moment longer on his arm. Just before placing old man Eli's head on the ground, The man had looked up at the heavens and said, 'Father, forgive them.' The man finally looked at them and told them they best be getting back so they would not get in trouble. He told them he would take care of burying old man Eli.

"He look' at us for a while Ms Mamie and says, 'member the ways of this good man. Think not of yo'sel'es, but others. For yo' Father in Heaven will bless you if you do this," Sam said with a very peaceful and understanding look in his eyes. "I's b'lieve him, Ms Mamie. I's *kno'* in my heart tha' man spok' the tru'h."

Thomas, nodding with the same understanding, spoke up. "'Nother thang he says, Ms Mamie," he turned and looked at

Sam as if unsure he should tell her. Sam nodded. "He says,"
he paused. "He says 'my *broth'rs*' to us." He again looked at
Sam for assurance that he too had heard the man. Sam nodded, his eyes misty with tears.

"He tre't us like we's be real peo'le; peo'le with feelin',"
Thomas said very appreciatively, and Sam nodded in agree-
ment. They smiled warmly as they stood to leave. Both gave
Mamie a hug and started for the door.

"Ms Mamie, tha' man sho' be dif'ent," Sam said quietly;
the way he said it again reminded Mamie of the time and way
old man Eli had said it, too.

"I's kno'," she said more to herself than to him.

Long after they had left Mamie sat at her old table deep in
thought. A feeling of apprehension went through her heart. If
the stranger was a minister of God, would he remain good and
kind? As much as Mamie wanted to believe he would, she
knew the others would soon tell him how he was to treat
slaves, and he would become mean to them, too. Though she
didn't want him to, she knew he would have to in order to be
accepted by his own kind.

Mamie got down on her knees and thanked the Lord for
what the kind stranger had done for her child and for old man

Eli. She asked him to bless the stranger to know that she had never felt or seen his kind of compassion before. Also to help him not feel bad when he learned he was not to be kind to them.

The days following Thomas and Sam's experience at the swamps brought many sorrows to them. Daily it seemed that they were beaten for seeking to help other slaves with their work. It seemed whenever one of the slaves needed help, one of them would stop their work and go to help, even though they would get into trouble with the overseer for doing so. Once Sam even rushed over to help the overseer when he was looking around on the ground for something.

"Kan I's help yous find sum'un s'ur?" he asked innocently.

At first the overseer looked shocked. He stared at Sam as if not sure he had heard him. The shock soon turned to anger as he yelled at Sam to get back to work.

After work that day, Mamie told Sam and Thomas to be careful. Lately she had been feeling fear for them, feeling like something awful was going to happen. She warned them that they should just do what Massa and the overseer wanted them to do no matter how much one of the other slaves might need their help. They both nodded as if they completely understood and would follow her advice, yet the very next day nothing had changed; they acted as if they hadn't heard a word she had said.

The overseer started treating them even more cruelly. It was as if he now looked for any reason to strike them with his whip. Mamie began praying real hard day and night for the good Lord to help them not do things to give the overseer a reason to beat them. She even prayed and asked the Lord that if they could not stop helping others, to at least shield them so that the overseer could not see the things they did or to have the overseer think they were crazy in the head and couldn't help themselves.

For a while Mamie felt her prayers were being answered. Though they had continued to leave their work and help others, the overseer always acted as if he did not see them. Then one day they both left their work to go help a couple of older women who had fallen behind in their work.

The one woman named Sage had a particularly bad back and found it difficult to bend over and straighten back up. Many times in the evening after work she had to walk back to her shack unable to stand straight. Grace, the woman with her, had bad ankles. Her ankles were swollen badly, and being an extremely big woman, made it hard for her to stand or walk. Usually she sat on the ground and dragged herself forward as she worked.

Mamie felt both were too ill to be working, but her feelings didn't matter, nor did theirs.

When Mamie saw Sam and Thomas leaving their work to go help Sage and Grace, she looked to see if the overseer was watching them. He was. He took off his hat and stared at them for a few seconds. He then shook his head as if he did not want to believe his eyes.

Mamie had barely turned to look at Sam and Thomas when something rushed past her. It was the overseer. He had moved so quickly toward them that even she was completely startled. With his whip, he repeatedly lashed their backs.

As Mamie listened to the sound of the whip lashing into them, she waited for another sound to come. It didn't. Both Sam and Thomas lay on the ground taking the fast, hard blows as they came but neither made a sound. Though their blood was clearly visible to all that were there, the two made no plea for mercy.

Mamie could not stand it any longer. Dropping to her knees, she began pleading with the overseer on their behalf. Soon, all the slaves were on their knees begging him to have mercy. Yelling at them to shut up, he finally stopped.

The overseer looked weary, even irritated, as he stopped his beating. He then rode a short distance away and looked back in their direction as if he had fought a battle and *lost*. There was no anger on his face; just a look of utter defeat and confusion. Before riding off, however, he had ordered Sam and Thomas to lie there and not move until quitting time. The other slaves were ordered not to go near them, not even to give them water.

It was obvious that they were suffering as they lay there, their wounds exposed to the heat of the sun, but they gave no indication of it. Having gone through the agony of not being allowed to have water, Mamie knew somewhat of the pain they were going through, but she could not and did not fully comprehend the extent of their suffering; she had not had open flesh wounds exposed to the hot rays of the sun. In spite of their predicament, she could not understand why they still did not make a sound or facially give any indication to the degree of their affliction.

Mamie's tears, as well as the tears of other slaves, flowed steadily for them as they worked. She wanted desperately to hand them a cup of water or do something to shield them from the hot sun, but her fear was greater. She looked up at the sky and knew that it was hopeless to pray for rain, yet she held strongly to a feeling of the truthfulness of old man Eli's words that 'all things be possible with the good Lord.' Realizing she badly needed the Lord's help, she prayed to him for them; asking him to somehow ease their suffering.

Mamie had barely ended her prayer when the overseer yelled that it was time for a water break. She thought about how old man Eli had gone without water when she could not have it and decided to do the same for Sam and Thomas. She was about to continue with her work when Jesse, one of the youngest children in the field, walked past her with a cup full of water. She felt her heart fill with fear when she realized he was headed straight for Sam and Thomas.

Carefully kneeling, Jesse took his free little hand, raised Sam's head, and let him drink slowly from the cup. When Sam indicated he had had enough, Jesse took what was left, poured it into his small hand and wet Sam's face. He then walked back over to the pail, refilled the cup, and did the same to Thomas. As he started to walk away, both Sam and Thomas said thank you. Jesse smiled warmly and shrugged his shoulders as if he hadn't done anything unusual. Realizing she had not had the courage of that small child, Mamie felt tremendous shame come over her.

Mamie looked in the overseer's direction to see what was going to happen next. He sat looking in their direction but it was as if completely unaware of what the child had just done. She looked at little Jesse, now busy at his work, and wondered if he had feared what could have happened to him. If he did, he did not show it. He appeared totally oblivious to the physical harm he could have brought upon himself.

After work a group of the slaves carried Sam and Thomas to their shacks. Mamie went to tend to Sam's wounds while another slave woman went to take care of Thomas's. She was busy washing the dirt from Sam's open wounds when little Jesse entered the shack and handed her a small jar. Mamie looked at him and then at it. The small jar looked familiar, and, for a brief moment, she puzzled over where she had seen it or one like it before.

"Where did yous get this?" Mamie asked Jesse, trying to recall why it looked so familiar.

"A white man gives it to me and says to tell yous to rub it on thay wounds," Jesse answered turning to leave.

"Wait," Mamie called out to him, apparently too loudly because he jumped as he turned and looked at her with a frightened look on his face.

"The man, was it Massa or the overseer?" She asked.

"No," he said as he again turned to leave.

"Son," she said, trying to be calm. "Pleas', tell me, *who* was it then tha' gave yous this jar?"

He looked at her as if surprised by her question.

"God's friend," he stated emphatically.

Speechless, Mamie nodded her head, and he left.

"It be him." Mamie heard Sam say weakly from behind her. She did not know he had been listening. She turned to look at him, and he was looking at her with a gentle smile on his face.

"It be's him, Ms Mamie," he repeated. "The man down at the swamps when old man Eli died, I's *kno'* it be him."

Mamie stared at the small jar in her hand and then at Sam.

"I's feel yous be righ', Sam. I's jus' don't kno' why he be kind to us," she said as she opened the jar and began rubbing some of it on Sam's wounds.

"Ms Mamie, I's think he be a friend of God like lit'le Jesse says, 'cept I's b'lieve he be not jus' eny friend, but one chose' and put here on this earth," Sam said with a very peaceful look on his face. "I's b'lieve he be 'pecial 'cause he be kind to *us* too and not jus' white folk'. That man was migh'y kind to old man Eli that day at the swamp. He make me b'lieve he be like the good Lord be."

Mamie sat down on the floor near Sam's bed and sighed heavily. "Sam I's b'lieves as you's do," she said. She then told him about her other encounters with the stranger.

"I's b'lieves he be of God and he be a *good* man of God but only 'cause he be new," Mamie said. "I's fears greatly that he will change. I's get heartsick each time I's finds myself thinkin' he real'y care' 'bout us. I's want so badly to b'lieve he care', but I's scare' to. It hurt' to b'lieve in him and at the same time kno' tha' time soon be changin' him."

"I's 'spect yous be righ' tha' he soon change when he be with those other preach'rs," Sam added sadly.

Nodding in agreement, Mamie said good night and stood to leave.

"Ms Mamie, do yous think we's kan pray for him; kan we's ask the good Lord not to let him be's like them others, and he won't?" Sam asked, his voice sounding very depressed, yet hopeful.

"Old man Eli once told me that all thangs be pos'ble with the good Lord," Mamie said. "We's kan only pray and see if the good Lord will hear our prayers." She paused and then chuckled. "'Course, the good Lord migh' wonder why we's be prayin' for tha' white man when we's need all the help we's kan get for oursel's."

Sam smiled; his face showing what Mamie was hoping it would—encouragement..

As Mamie stepped outside, she looked up at heaven. It was practically covered with stars and looked so very peaceful.

"Good Lord, why kant we's be like all those stars up there; thay's each have a place to shine brigh'. Why kant we's be like tha' down here?" She whispered quietly, greatly in awe by the number and appearance of harmony among the stars.

Thomas's and Sam's wounds seemed to heal rapidly. As soon as they had completely recovered, a wagon showed up at the shacks, and they were told that their new owner was there to collect them.

The slaves were all devastated by the news, yet knew that all they could do was accept it. When they were loaded on the wagon to be taken away, many were shedding tears, including Mamie. Sam and Thomas also looked heartbroken, but neither let any tears fall as they sought to remain very self-composed. Mamie's heart filled with pride; she knew they were seeking to be strong for those left behind.

Sam held out his hand to Mamie as he settled on the wagon. Seeing him do this made her recall her children and how both had held out their tiny hand, too. Her sobs became uncontrollable.

"Don't yous cry, Ms Mamie," Sam said solemnly. "I's wont forgit yous. I's 'member you's always in my heart. Yous been like a mammy to me, and I's thank the good Lord. Someday..." he paused, and she felt certain he was trying to hold back his tears. "Someday, I's promise yous, I's gon' come back and see yous; I's gon' make sho' yous be okay," he said as his eyes gradually filled with tears.

Wanting him to know he was loved, Mamie reached down and untied the string around her ankle with her wood chip on it.

"Sam, I's want yous to have this," she said. She was in the process of handing the wood chip to him when the man who had bought them grabbed her hand and stared intently at the wood chip dangling from it.

"Where did you get this?" He asked bitterly as he stared at her coldly.

"It be mine; I's made it years ago," she said.

"You sure you didn't get this from a runaway slave?" He asked angrily.

"No s'ur. It be mine," she repeated, puzzled by his attitude.

"Well, it sure looks like one a slave I bought had. The dirty, one armed nigger. My parents practically raised him after he almost died from a gunshot wound and all the thanks he could give was to run away. Can't trust *any* of you." He said with deep hostility and then walked back to the front of the wagon.

Still puzzled over what had just happened, Mamie placed the wood chip in Sam's hand, trying not to let the man's words ruin her final moments with him.

"It's all I's got, but I's like for yous to have it to remind yous that yous be love as my own son. Whenever yous feel lonely, jus' rub it and kno' that I's be thinkin' 'bout yous," Mamie said as she gave him a hug.

"Thank yous, Ms Mamie. I's keep it always." he said, no longer trying to control his tears. She held his hand until the wagon pulled away.

"Bye, Ms Mamie," Sam said with a warm, peaceful look in his eyes. He was about to say more but the wagon moved away too swiftly. He waved as tears flowed freely down his face. A look of great sadness showed as well. She couldn't help but feel his sadness and tears were more for them than for himself.

Mamie could hear the sobs of those around her. She looked to see Sage and Grace crying terribly as each tried to console the other. They all knew the great loss their lives would feel without those two.

Mamie stood watching the dust from the wagon long after it was out of view. A very familiar feeling of having stood and watched another wagon do the *same* thing, filled her heart with greater sorrow.

"How many mo' times must my h'art be to'n 'part, good Lord?" She whispered quietly as the last view of dust settled.

A few days later word came that Thomas or Sam had been killed when the wagon they were riding in overturned and crushed one of them underneath.

Yet there was something in his eyes
That won my love, I knew not why

Chapter Three

Not Forgotten

That following winter was a particularly difficult one for everyone. The crops had done poorly and a lot of animals died from diseases. Massa even started selling off a lot of the slaves to keep food on his own table. Before the winter was half over, he and his wife left to go spend the rest of it with her family. They told the slaves they were going for a *friendly* visit, but everyone knew it was to escape the pitiable situation they were in.

The snow was unrelenting as it continued to fall day and night. As the nights grew longer and the weather became increasingly bitter, the little food the slaves had quickly dwindled away. Even wood to burn became increasingly difficult to find. Many of them moved in with other slaves to save on fire wood and to combine what meager food they had left. In spite of all their efforts to combine their means to make it through that winter, many still died, mostly young children.

Late one evening as Mamie sat holding Jesse, who was very ill, he stared up at her with frightened, tear-filled eyes.

"Ms Mamie," he said. "I's be real scare'."

"Why child?" Mamie asked him as she pulled him closer to her heart and rubbed his bony forehead.

"'Cause I's gon' die," he said, his eyes filled with tears. "I's real scare'."

"You's not gon' die child," she said. "You's gon' be 'round a long time, a migh'y long time."

He shook his head.

"Naw I's not, Ms Mamie."

His words and eyes told Mamie he spoke the truth, but her heart refused to accept it.

"'Member the time yous give Thomas and Sam water as thay lay in the hot sun all bleedin' from ol' overseer's beatin'?" Mamie asked, trying to cheer him up.

He nodded his head.

"Well the good Lord's not gon' let yous die; yous got lots mo' folks to help," she said.

"Naw I's not, Ms Mamie," he repeated, shaking his head sadly. As he spoke, a really strange feeling went through Mamie this time. She stared at him for a few minutes before speaking.

"How's yous kno' yous gon' die?" She asked him. "Yous wantin' to lea'e me?"

His eyes never left hers as he continued staring at her with an extremely sad look on his face. "I's kno' cause I's be told so. I's be told not to be scare', but I's still is."

Mamie stared at him and then closed her eyes as she drew him close to her heart and held him there for a long time. Finally she looked back into his eyes.

"Jesse, don't yous be 'fraid to die. The good Lord gon' be waitin' for yous, and he gon' put his arms 'round yous and keep yous safe and warm fo'ever," she said, trying desperately to hold back her tears.

"The good Lord love' me, Ms Mamie?" he asked. "I's want to be love'."

"Yous love' child. I's love yous *and* the good Lord love' yous. Do yous 'member yo' mammy child?" Mamie asked him.

"I's ne'er had a mammy," he said sadly.

"Yous got a mammy child; we all got a mammy even if we's ne'er kno' who she be, but wherever yo' mammy be, she loves yous."

He did not say anything as he continued staring at her.

"Ms Mamie, will the good Lord give me a good apple when he put his arms 'round me?" He asked.

Mamie's heart broke as she looked into his little, lonely eyes and saw all the pain his heart carried. She knew he was thinking about all the times he and other slave children had spent hours picking all the big, red apples from the trees for Massa, only to be given the ones with worms in them or ones that were rotten. Many times some of them would try to sneak a good one away only to be caught and given a good beating.

"Oh, yes he's will, Jesse. The good Lord gon' give yous the best there be. He's saw how hard yous work' for it, and yous gon' finally get to pick the best there be," Mamie said as she squeezed him close. He closed his eyes with a big smile on his face.

Mamie leaned her head back on the old chair and closed her eyes. She tried to picture herself standing before the good Lord and asking him why they were treated so badly; why didn't he do something to help, especially for the children.

Tears began flowing from her closed eyes, but she quickly opened them so the tears would stop. She didn't want little Jesse to see them; she knew she needed to be strong for his sake.

Looking down at him resting peacefully, Mamie began to hum as she gently rocked him. He opened his eyes and smiled.

"I's not 'fraid to die enymo', Ms Mamie," he said smiling as he closed his eyes again.

"Tha's good child," Mamie said. "But I's don't think yous gon' die. Yous gon' be runnin' and playin' when tha' snow goes 'way and the sun warms the earth agin." She kissed his forehead and continued humming and rocking him late into the night. It was not until she went to put him down that she realized he was dead; the smile still on his face.

That winter continued to be a long hard one. Mamie often wondered if any of them would make it through alive. There was no longer any food to eat nor wood to burn. There was no hope of their situation changing until the weather changed, and it was evident that most of them would not last that long.

One night as they all sat huddled together to keep warm, a knock came at the door. At first Mamie wasn't sure she had heard it and looked around to see if any of the other slaves were acting as if they had noticed it. Some of them were looking at each other. Soon the sound came again, more forceful this time.

"Lord have mercy; who it be out in this weather?" One of the old slave men said as he stood to go see. "Whoever it be, be righ' crazy to be out in this weather," he said as he opened the door. The slaves huddled closer as the cold wind came gushing in. In stepped three white men. In spite of the slaves' pitiful condition, fear gripped their hearts. Mamie started praying as they all huddled closer together.

"Please, don't fear," one of the men said as he removed the scarf that hid most of his face. Even before his scarf had been completely removed, Mamie recognized the voice to be that of the kind, tall stranger.

As they closed the door behind them, she tried to see what it was they were carrying under their arms. The kind, tall stranger and the other men with him placed the bundles before the slaves, who quickly began opening them. Mamie shook her head in disbelief when she saw what was inside them: food, blankets, water, and in one, pieces of wood. Her heart filled with joy as she closed her eyes and thanked the good Lord for the men's goodness. She then looked at the kind, tall stranger to say 'thank you' but he shook his head no.

"These things come from many who know of and are concerned about your suffering. They, like me, wish we could do more," he said. He then said good night and started for the door.

"Mr." Mamie quietly called out to him as he was leaving. He turned and looked at her. "Who's be yous?" She asked.

He stopped, looked at her, and stared down at the floor for a brief moment before looking at her again. It was at that moment that Mamie thought about a story old man Eli had told them about how one of the Lord's servants had asked him who he was and the Lord had said, "Who do you say I am?" Her heart began to pound mightily as she stared at him.

"Mr," Mamie softly whispered. "Yous don't have to tell me."

Giving a gentle nod with his head, he turned and left. As he did, Mamie felt the love of the good Lord flow through her ever so warmly. His eyes conveyed to the heart, in its truest sense, the love of God. She thought how old man Eli had been right when he had said the man was different; he certainly was. Although he was still quite young, Mamie found herself feeling certain that he would not and could not become mean or cruel to *anyone*. His heart was truly pure.

When that long hard winter finally came to an end, Mamie learned that other slaves had received help from the three men. Many wondered who they were and why they were helping slaves, but no one had an answer. Although she had a strong feeling inside who the kind, tall stranger was, she said not a word.

Massa apparently learned that some men had helped them and went to every slave on the place trying to find out who they were. Like the other slaves, when he asked Mamie, she lied and told him she had never seen any of them before. He told them to let him know if they ever saw any of these men on his property again. Like the rest, she assured him she would but had no intention of doing so. She knew in her heart that she would never tell him the truth for fear he would try to have the kind, tall stranger destroyed for helping them. He finally stopped asking about them.

For a long time Mamie did not see the kind, tall stranger who had become a blessing of good-will to them. She didn't expect him to show up every time a crisis happened, because he didn't. He was there, however, more times than one would expect a person with no known obligation to be. Somehow, he just seemed to know when his help was most needed.

The slaves strived harder each day to help each other endure. One of the young mothers named Frances Ann reminded Mamie a lot of herself when she had her first child. The young mother had a newborn son named Isaac, and it was evident that he was her life. She seemed to grieve terribly each time she had to be away from him. As Mamie watched her becoming greatly attached to him, she tried to warn her about what was going to happen, though she felt the young mother already knew. Mamie understood how she felt. A mother's love could not be withheld from her child, even under the conditions of slavery and the never-ending heartbreaking knowledge that the child could be taken at any moment and sold.

When the slaves left for work one morning the sky overhead was clear, though dark clouds hung far off in a distance. By the time they got to the end farthest from the shacks the sky started changing rapidly. Mamie looked over at Frances Ann and could see the panic growing in her eyes. She constantly looked up at the sky and then in the direction of the shacks. Mamie knew she was thinking about her child and what could happen if it started to rain. The crippled woman who took care of the babies would not be able to get them all inside.

As the sky continued to grow darker, the concern of all the young mothers became evident. Frances Ann finally muscled up the courage to ask the overseer if she could go take the babies inside. He smirked at her question and never answered. She waited a few minutes and then asked him again. He stared at her for a few seconds and then gave another smirk.

"You better keep working 'fore you won't be able to take your *own* self in," he finally said.

She continued working, but Mamie could tell her mind wasn't on the work. Mamie saw her lips moving and knew she was praying. When a roar of thunder drowned out all sound, she let out a scream and again begged the overseer to please let her go take the babies inside. This time he showed his hostility and power as he told her if she asked again, he would *never* let her or any of them go in.

Out of fear for her safety, Mamie started praying she would not ask him again, but put her faith in the good Lord to look after those helpless little babies. Her body was shaking greatly and tears rolled down her cheeks. Mamie knew

Frances Ann wanted to keep an eye on the sky, but she didn't dare to. Mamie's heart ached for her, and she, too, began to cry.

All of a sudden, a very frightening and tumultuous sound roared across the sky; Mamie was so shaken by it, she screamed. As quickly as it came, every thick, black cloud above seemingly opened as rain poured forth upon them. *No one* waited for the overseer to tell them to leave. Screaming, they all broke into a mad run for the shacks. Frances Ann was in front of everyone, praying loudly to the Lord to save her child. She knew, as they all did, that it did not take long for those wash tubs to fill and drown those small babies.

Mamie moved as quickly as she could, which wasn't very fast. Grace, the lady with the swollen ankles, held tightly onto her arm. She wasn't able to run, but tried to move her feet as hurriedly as she could. Mamie feared they would never make it; she was certain Grace felt the same way. Mamie could hear her praying, asking the good Lord to please have mercy upon them. The rain was pounding so hard that several times Mamie had to stop to make sure they were headed in the right direction.

Mamie and Grace were not blessed to move faster, but out of nowhere two men appeared and helped them make it to the shacks. Mamie couldn't make out who they were due to the downpour and darkness of the sky, but her heart felt the depth of their heroic deed. When she realized they had made it home, she closed her eyes and thanked the good Lord. Feeling the hands of her helper no longer on her, she opened her eyes to thank whoever it was, but the person had disappeared into the storm. She turned toward Grace, thinking she could thank the person helping her, but he too was gone.

Mamie helped Grace to her shack and then hurried over to see the crippled woman. As she neared her shack, she could see the wash tubs still outside and filled with water. Not bothering to knock, Mamie pushed open the crippled woman's door. She was sitting on her bed, clothes completely dry and smiling happily.

"Ms Mamie," she said as she beckoned her inside. "Yous not gon' b'lieve what happen."

"Yous not wet," Mamie said, puzzled.

"Oh no," she said cheerfully. "I's be i'side fo' a lon' time."

"The babies," Mamie said. "What happ'n to them?"

"I's didn't get them i'side," she said smiling. Mamie was shocked by her words and actions and felt herself getting faint.

"A man did," the crippled woman continued. "I's tells yous, Ms Mamie, that man save those babies," she humbly stated.

Even before Mamie asked her next question, her heart had already told her who the crippled woman was talking about, but she had to know for sure.

"What man?" Mamie asked, her heart pounding.

"I's don't kno' who he be, but he be real kind," she said.

"The man," Mamie said, pausing to take a deep breath. "Was he a tall, white man?"

"He sho' 'nough was. In fact Ms Mamie, I's b'lieves he be the same one who brough' us food when we be starvin' that winter," she said. "And yous kno' sum'un else, Ms Mamie?"

Mamie shook her head as she silently thanked the good Lord for sending him again.

"He be real 'spectful and polite to *me*."

Mamie nodded and smiled as she saw how pleased and surprised the crippled woman was. Mamie briefly recalled how she had felt the day he had first shown up at her door; the shock she had felt over his speaking to her as if she had been someone deserving his respect.

"He sho' be dif'ent," the crippled woman said with the same tone of amazement as others who had seen and heard him.

Mamie told her she had to go get some dry rags on and left. As she stepped back outside into the storm, she again thanked the good Lord for sending the kind, tall stranger.

"Whoever he be," she said aloud, "he surely 'serves yo' best r'ward."

The next day Mamie tried to find the slaves who had helped Grace and her out of the storm to thank them but couldn't. She asked every male slave there if they had helped them but each one said no. Puzzled, she went and asked Grace if she had any idea who they were.

"Why Ms Mamie, yous be the only person who help me out of tha' awfa storm," she said. "Didn't no one else come help."

In spite of what Grace said, Mamie knew then and would forever *know* in her heart that someone else had helped them as well.

Not long after that storm, Frances Ann was sold. She cried and pleaded mightily with Massa as her son was taken from her arms and placed in those of the crippled woman.

Once, when my scanty meal was spread,
He entered; not a word he spake,
Just pershing for want of bread.
I gave him all; he blessed it, brake, And ate,

Chapter Four

The Master of Our Fate

As the weather grew warmer, the slaves stood outside until late in the night talking. News was rapidly spreading among them about a church that was baptizing slaves. A few of the slaves on Massa's place even sneaked off and were baptized.

The more Mamie heard about slaves getting baptized, the more she longed to go and do so, too. Each time she thought her mind was all made up to go, she'd talk herself out of doing it. She feared being caught by Massa and getting beat at her age. She therefore sought hard to put the notion of getting baptized out of her mind, which proved impossible.

Unable to rid herself of the notion, Mamie finally decided to go do it no matter what happened. She even told herself

Massa might be merciful and not beat her so terribly because of her age, even though she knew mercy would be the last thing to enter his mind.

The very night Mamie was getting ready to leave, she heard a lot of commotion outside. She could also hear someone crying loudly and pitifully. She stepped outside to see what was wrong and was surprised to find most of the slaves standing near a shack on the opposite side of hers. She had barely started toward them when Massa and the overseer came riding quickly up to where the slaves were standing. They got down off their horses and disappeared into the circle.

As Mamie neared the crowd, she could see that Massa and the overseer were looking down at a young slave boy named Luke, who looked as if he had been beaten and then dragged unconscious. Seeing him lying there in that condition made her mind flashed back to the day old man Eli had been dragged from his shack looking the same way.

She felt herself getting sick to her stomach at the condition of the boy and its reminder. Mamie covered her mouth to suppress the ghastly feeling within her.

Not far from Luke, kneeling on the ground, was his mother. It had been her mournful crying Mamie had heard. The mother was now looking hopelessly at Massa, crying and pleading with him to have mercy upon her son.

Mamie quietly asked the slave next to her what the boy had done. Looking frightened, she whispered that he had been caught coming from being baptized.

Massa got back on his horse and bellowed out orders to two of the slaves to build a fire. The mother, upon hearing this, began crying and pleading sorrowfully to Massa not to harm her son more, but her cries for mercy were to no avail. Massa sat on his horse staring straight ahead, looking as if she did not even exist.

When the flames grew large and bright and more intense, Mamie could clearly see Massa's face. The look was one of absolute rage. Her heart broke for the poor boy; she knew his suffering had only just begun.

Massa finally ordered another slave to tie Luke to the tree nearest the fire. He then nodded his head at the overseer, who by now was back on his horse, too. As the overseer rode slowly toward the boy, Massa told them if they had some crazy notion of doing what the boy had done they best forget it.

"No amount of water or religion is going help save your soul if *I* catch you," he yelled with a look of indignation. "The only saving your dirty souls will ever see is whatever I grant it. *I* am the *only* master you will ever have that can grant you mercy and save your soul, *if you have a soul.*" He paused as he glared at them. The overseer sat looking at them and gave an unrestrained sneering sound when Massa said, "if you have a soul."

Massa then nodded at the overseer to commence whipping the boy. His poor mother fainted and Mamie was grateful that she had. She didn't think the mother's heart would have been able to watch the many similar hard blows that followed.

When the overseer finally stopped, a very eerie feeling hung in the air.

"As your master, I decide whether you live or die," Massa said. "As this boy's master, I have decided to let him live, but the next time I catch one of you doing a fool thing like he did, I *will not* spare your life. I will show *no* mercy," he shouted loudly, his voice echoing in the stillness of the night. With a look of wrath on his face, he rode self-righteously past them and into the darkness of the night. The overseer followed him, but not until he gave one last hard merciless blow with his whip to the boy's legs.

"Why don't some more of you go get baptized?" he asked sarcastically. He then started laughing and rode off. Mamie looked at Luke's mother and thanked the good Lord she was not able to see the condition of her son. Her own flesh ached as she looked at that boy against the tree. She almost wished Massa had not spared his life; feeling certain there was very little of it left.

A few of the slave men went, cut Luke loose and took him inside his mother's shack. Mamie rushed to her shack to get some rags to help clean and tie together the flesh that lay open. When she got back, most of the slaves could not bare to look at him and were unable to clean his wounds. She knew it had to be done, so she knelt down by him and tried to gently pull the torn flesh together in order to tie it with a rag, but the slightest touch made him groan in agony. Some of the gashes were so deep that even the bones were severed. For hours Mamie worked, trying to stop his bleeding, feeling with each passing second that she was fighting a losing battle.

"May I come in?" someone said.

Mamie immediately turned to see who had said those words, and there he stood. Just outside the door was the kind, tall stranger and another man. Her heart felt greatly relieved though doubtful that there was anything he could do. She rose at once from beside the bed and said yes. She indicated with her arms for the other slaves to move and let them in. As they moved toward the boy, she wanted to tell him there was nothing he could do this time to help; that there was no way possible he could ease the boy's suffering, but didn't.

As the kind, tall stranger neared Luke and could clearly see the boy's open flesh, he turned his head and moaned. Then, kneeling on the floor next to the boy's head, he and the man with him placed their hands gently on the boy's bloody head and the kind, tall stranger began to pray.

With her eyes closed tightly, Mamie listened to him call upon the Lord in a way that made her tears fall. His words touched her heart ever so deeply and she felt a presence in the room that was strong and loving. He prayed for the boy *and* for those who had beaten him. His love for *all* people was indisputable. He cared deeply, about those who were free *and* those in bondage. He prayed for love and understanding between all mankind as he asked the good Lord to soften the hearts of those who had people in captivity. A number of times he had to pause and Mamie felt certain it was to control the grief that seemed to choke back his words. The feeling in the room was one her soul would not forget no matter how long she lived in captivity.

When he finished praying, a great silence hung over the room. Luke lay resting peacefully, his breathing flowing freely. Mamie watched as he gently stroked the boy's forehead. Shaking his head sadly, he rose to his feet.

Mamie had barely started moving toward him to thank him for coming and for his prayer when she felt someone push past her. She looked down to see Solomon, a young child of seven or eight, walking with his fist tightly folded toward the men. Stopping right in front of the kind, tall stranger, Solomon glared at him angrily.

"I's hate yous white folks," the boy yelled up at the man.

The kind, tall stranger looked at the boy as he knelt down to look directly at the child. He reached out to take one of the boy's hands, but the boy quickly pulled it back.

"Don't yous dare touch me. I's *HATE* yous," Solomon screamed in the kind, tall stranger's face.

"To hate is *wrong*," he said quietly to Solomon.

"Kant be, cause Massa and the overseer, and all yous white folks hates us," Solomon said, slightly raising his fist, and for a moment Mamie really felt he wanted to strike the kind, tall stranger. His little eyes and voice showed so much pain and anger.

"God wants *no* man to hate. God...." whatever he was going to say was abruptly interrupted by the boy.

"Don't yous tell me 'bout no God. Even he tells Massa and the overseer to be mean to us; to beat us if we's don't obey them. So don't yous tell me 'bout it be wrong to hate or what *God* wants. Thay and God no care 'bout me, and I's no care 'bout *them*," Solomon said as he then tried to turn and run, but the kind, tall stranger grabbed him and gently pulled him securely into his arms.

"The Lord wants *no* man to hate, not even your master," he said to the boy. "Hate is wrong, very wrong. And the Lord would *never* have your master be mean to you. Never!"

"But the Lord he not over me and the things Massa do; he be not my massa. Massa says he be the *only* master we have," the child said, his anger was still very evident.

"Sometimes men make themselves out to be more than they are. Your Massa only means he is over you while you are his servant. The Lord did say, '*Servants obey your master.*' The Lord, with his great wisdom and love, was trying to protect you. He does not want you to suffer," the stranger calmly replied.

"I's don't b'lieve you," Solomon said as he turned his head away from the kind, tall stranger. The man slowly turned his head back toward him and looked the boy tenderly in the eyes.

"Do you know what else the Lord said?" The stranger said to him. Solomon shook his head no.

"He said, '*He that is greatest among you shall be your servant.*' Greatest!" He emphasized this strongly to the boy. "Do you know what that means?"

"I's somebod' 'portant, too?" the boy asked, his voice sounding hopeful that he was right.

"*Yes,*" the stranger said with much excitement in his voice as he gave the boy a hug; a hug Solomon did not withdraw from.

"Son, always know how important you are to the Lord. Do you know something else the Lord said?" The boy again shook his head.

"He said, '*Blessed are ye when men shall persecute you; rejoice and be glad; for great is your reward in heaven, for so....*" the kind, tall stranger paused as if it was difficult for him to say more.

"*So persecuted they the prophets,*" the stranger was finally able to quietly and poignantly whisper.

Solomon slowly reached out, as if seeing the stranger for the first time, and touched his face. The stranger pulled the boy gently to his heart and held him there and wept. The boy wrapped his tiny arms around the kind, tall stranger's neck and started crying. "I's sorry yous be p'secuted," Solomon said. Mamie gasped, wondering why Solomon would say such a thing to the stranger, but the kind, tall stranger did not react nor correct him. Watching them, her own tears began to fall.

The kind, tall stranger finally held the boy back and looked into his eyes. With a voice that sounded ever so warm and full of love, he said, "Little one, you are the salt of the earth, but if you *hate* because you are hated, you will be henceforth good for nothing." He was silent for a moment as the boy nodded his head with understanding. "Be a *light* to the world and shine brightly so that men might see your love and the good things you do and glorify your Father who is in heaven."

"I's try real hard," Solomon said. "Real hard." He and the man were quiet as they looked at each other. The boy put his arms back around the kind, tall stranger's neck and gave him a hug.

"I know you will," the kind, tall stranger smiled and said, "It won't be easy, but let no man make you stoop to his level. Be strong and know that what matters most is what your Father in heaven thinks of you." The boy nodded, smiling happily.

The two men nodded to Mamie and started toward the door. They were about to step outside when Solomon ran forward and pulled at the kind, tall stranger's arm.

"Mr, will yous bap'ize me, too?" Solomon softly cried out to him. Surprised by his words again, Mamie frowned and opened her mouth to offer an apology for the boy's bad manners, but the stranger held up his hand to silence her as he knelt before Solomon.

"I cannot, little one, at least not for a small while," he said very earnestly, and there was great sadness in his eyes.

"Why not?" Solomon asked, his voice sounding as if he was about to cry.

"Remember how I said the Lord wants to protect you?" Solomon nodded his head.

"Well, so that no more mistreatment comes to you and your people because of their choosing to follow God's will to be baptized, the Lord wants me to wait until the day when you can freely make the decision to be baptized without the risk and fear of getting beaten by *any* man on this earth."

"But I's never gon' be free, so I's ne'er gon' git bap'ized," Solomon said sadly.

The man looked for a moment into Solomon's eyes and then stared at the floor for a moment. Finally looking back into the boy's eyes as if he was seeing far into the future he spoke.

"I *promise* you, little one, the day will come when you *will* be free from the chains of slavery; free to follow God's will and plan according to the dictates of your *own* heart."

Mamie gasped loudly, and the man with the kind, tall stranger looked questionably down at him and then at Mamie.

She looked at the child standing calmly before the stranger; saw the hope that brought a brightness to his face, and her heart broke. She felt deep anger and disappointment toward the stranger. She could not understand how he could lie to an innocent little child.

Mamie moved toward them and slowly pulled Solomon from in front of the stranger and into her arms.

"I's think yous better be gon', s'ur," she said. Mamie made sure the tone of her voice and the look in her eyes was cold to let him know her disappointment with him and the foolish thing he had just told Solomon.

The stranger stood and stared back into Mamie's eyes. In spite of the great hurt and disappointment she felt toward him, she could see he meant no harm. She swallowed hard as she plainly knew he understood the suffering they were going through and in no way would ever do anything to increase that suffering, yet, she still felt it was wrong of him to give false hope, especially to an innocent child.

He looked down at Solomon and then back at Mamie.

"Have *faith*. Freedom *will* come; it will come," he said in what was barely a whisper but so very powerful and sincere.

He patted the boy gently on the head and left. He was barely out the door when Solomon looked up at Mamie.

"Ms Mamie, I's b'lieve him; I's b'lieve I's be free someday; and when I's am, I's gon' be bap'ized," he said.

Mamie wanted to tell Solomon that she would like to believe that freedom would come, but her heart was too afraid to hope for something she knew never would. She smiled at the boy and nodded; if only he knew how badly she wanted to believe, too.

Mamie told Solomon he best get to his shack as she went to check on Luke. He was still resting peacefully. She then walked outside to head for her shack. The fire Massa had made was practically out. She shivered as she looked over at the tree where Luke had been tied. She looked at the heavens and was saddened to see that there were no stars out tonight. "Lord, I's un'erstan' why," she whispered quietly to the dark night.

The next morning things were as they always were. Though the blood on the tree was clearly visible to remind them what had happened, Mamie chose to ignore it; the pain of facing what had happened was simply too great. The overseer was the only one who stopped in front of it and snickered.

For weeks after that night, things were quiet. Luke's wounds healed beautifully, and he was soon ordered back to the fields. Then one day while walking to work, without any warning that he was sick or hurting in any way, he stumbled from side to side a couple of times and then fell to the ground. Within seconds, he was dead. He apparently had had some internal injuries that they were not aware of, but even if they had known, there was nothing they could have done.

His death was so sudden and so unexpected that his mother's heart just could not take it. Within days she too passed away. One slave said it was due to a broken heart. The slave went on to say the mother had said before she died that she had no regrets for her son's decision to be baptized, and he still would have done it even if he had known it would be followed by the awful beating Massa had the overseer give him. The mother could not understand why Massa had ordered the beating for something so harmless; she just could not understand what was wrong with getting baptized. Mamie tried to understand but couldn't, none of them could. She finally concluded that maybe it was because he thought they would look to someone other than him as being more important, or maybe he just did not want them thinking baptism was for slaves. Try as she might, Mamie just could not find an answer. Her only comfort in the senseless beating of Luke was gained when she thought about how old man Eli had once said, *"He's that lose his life for the good Lord, shall find it."*

It took some time for the slaves' hearts to stop hurting over Luke's and his mother's death. Mamie's heart felt a terrible pain every time she saw that tree or Massa. Seeing Massa made her think of the night he had said he was the *only* one who decided whether they lived or died. She wanted so badly to ask him if it was *his* decision to have Luke die. She simply wanted to let him know that she knew he did not always control death.

As awful treatment toward them continued, Mamie found herself wondering if Massa had somehow heard what the kind, tall stranger had told them about freedom. It seemed he was doing all he could to discourage any thinking they might have about someday being free, or that there was a Savior who cared about them. In spite of the dark hours and days they faced, she did not forget the kind, tall stranger's words for them to '*have faith.*' It was indeed faith she held onto day and night.

...but gave me part again.
Mine was but an angel's portion then,

Chapter Five

Fatal Choices

Massa finally took away the one little comfort of strength the slaves' hearts relied on to help them make it through all the harsh treatment their souls were forced to endure; he forbade them to gather to sing and pray to the good Lord. It happened on a night when they had had a tremendously tormenting day. Though their bodies ached mightily, their spirits hungered more. As they were on their way to meet to sing praises and to ask for the good Lord's strength to better endure their trials, Massa and the overseer came riding up. Mamie was sure they knew where the slaves were going and why, yet Massa asked anyway. One of the slaves, smiling, told him they were headed to sing praises to the good Lord.

"Sing praises to the good Lord," Massa said mockingly. He looked at the overseer, and they both chuckled.

"Why would you be wanting to sing praises to the 'good' Lord?" He asked the slave, making it seem as if they were doing something very foolish. The slave realized what was going on and stopped smiling as fear quickly spread across his face. He looked nervously around at the rest of the slaves.

"I's don't kno', s'ur," he said, his voice quivering. "We's be happy yous keep us, and we's gon' go thank the good Lord for yo' kindness," he said.

The slaves all knew he was lying, but they nodded their head and smiled happily at Massa. For a moment Mamie thought he believed them as he sat for a few seconds looking pleased. When he burst out laughing, she knew his rage would be forth coming.

"Don't you niggers try to make a fool of me," he said, and from the tone of his voice, Mamie knew that some of them would not live to see the morning sun. He raised his foot and kicked the slave who had been talking to him squarely in the chest as the overseer kicked the one nearest him in the back. The slaves all scattered and started running to their shacks as Massa screamed at them.

"Don't you ever let me hear of you getting together again unless *I* tell you to," he said vehemently, his voice rising clearly above the noise. He rode his horse toward a slave who was trying to make it to his shack. When he caught up with the slave, he allowed his horse to knock the slave over. "Do I make myself clear?" He shouted.

Mamie rushed inside her shack and latched the door, knowing that if he ordered her to come out she would. Her heart pounding rapidly, Mamie waited and listened for the sound of their horses leaving so she could go out and see if the slave Massa's horse had knocked over was hurt.

As Mamie waited to hear the sound of them leaving, she found herself feeling ashamed and angry at all of them for not being willing to stand up to Massa. They were doing nothing wrong in wanting to sing and pray together. They never allowed anything to interfere with their faithfully doing Massa's work everyday.

For a brief moment Mamie found herself wanting to go out and die for something that meant so much to her. She wanted to walk out her door and say, *"Massa, I's aims to get with the other slaves and sing praises to the good Lord no matter what yous do to me."* But no sooner had she finished the thought did the fear become greater than the courage to fight.

While Mamie stood there by her door trembling, she felt so ashamed. Old man Eli would have been very disappointed in them. He had always said to them at the end of each meeting, "Y'all mus' always 'member that the good Lord said, *'And if ye suffa for righ'eous'ess sake, happy are ye; and be not 'fraid of their terror, nei'her be trouble'.*"

It was not until they had left that someone went outside and saw that Grace had fallen and been trampled to death. When Mamie learned of her death, she felt horrible for having failed to help her along when it had been she who had talked Grace into going with them. Grace had said no when Mamie first asked her—saying her ankles were terribly sore. Mamie had told her a little praying and singing was just what her ankles needed. Though Grace still hadn't wanted to go, she had smiled trustingly at Mamie and followed her.

"Well, Ms Mamie, if yous think the good Lord will give me jus' a lit'le 'lief from all this here pain I's be havin', I's gla'ly go," she had said cheerfully as she reached for Mamie's arm. She had been hanging onto her when Mamie became frightened of what Massa was going to do to them, pulled lose from her grip and ran.

Mamie prayed hard that night that Grace would forgive her. Her heart sorrowed all the more as she recalled old man Eli telling them to love each other and even be willing to die for each other. He told them how Christ had said that '*no greater love hath no man than to lay down his life for a friend.*' Mamie knew she had not been such a friend to Grace, or she would have helped her get inside or died trying.

Grace's death and being unable to get together made Mamie's heart feel absolutely miserable. She hadn't realized how much those meetings meant to her until they were no longer able to have them. She needed to share the pains of her heart and have help to carry on. Unfortunately, Massa had taken that source of strength from them.

Late one night as Mamie sat outside she found herself thinking about the fatal choices of so many. The fatal choice of her son who had only wanted to return to his mother; the choice of old man Eli, who had only wanted a few days to rest and to get better, but had not *earned* the time to do so in spite of all the years of hard work he had given unto Massa; Luke, who had just wanted the joy and peace of being baptized; Grace, who had only wanted to go sing and pray for relief for her paining ankles; and others who had died simply because they each made an innocent choice that had not been approved by Massa or the overseer.

"Dear Lord, please sho' me the righ' choice I's kan make for yous. I's don't mind how hard the road migh' be, jus' help me kno' I's doin' righ' with my life down here on this earth," Mamie cried out into the stillness of the night.

For while I fed with eager hast,
The crust was manna to my taste.

Chapter Six

The Book

Early one hot summer morning Massa and the overseer left for business in another town and would be gone for a few days. The slaves immediately made plans to get together that evening. As the day passed, Mamie found it very difficult to wait for the sky to darken.

When they finally gathered, little Solomon lead them in a song. Looking overjoyed, he rose to his feet and began singing. He then asked Mamie to read a word to them from the Bible old man Eli had given her. Although she had always carried it to the meetings with her, she had only opened it the night old man Eli had given it to her; seeing all those letters had frightened her.

Only the crackling of the fire could be heard as all eyes stared at Mamie. Her heart pounded greatly with fear as she thought about old man Eli and how he could not read either, yet he always had a story from the Bible to tell them each time they gathered. Once a slave stood up after old man Eli had finished one of his Bible stories and said, "How's yous kno' that story be in there, yous kant read like the rest of us kant."

Old man Eli had been quiet for a moment as he stared down at the ground. Mamie had felt sorry for him; for they all knew he couldn't read, but they enjoyed the things he shared with them and they never questioned them; his words sounded so real, so right.

Old man Eli looked at the slave with a very painful and sad expression on his face.

"I's kno' cause the good Lord reads to me. He speak' the words to my heart," he said firmly.

He then told them how Moses had been slow of speech and the Lord had taught him what to say. He also told them about Solomon and how the Lord gave him wisdom and understanding.

"And it be the good Lord who gives me un'stan'in', too," he said.

Mamie remembered sitting there and feeling so strongly how important old man Eli was; he had the good Lord helping him to read and understand. No one ever again questioned the things old man Eli shared.

She now looked down at his old Bible with the realization that old man Eli had been special to the Lord; she wasn't. Mamie was about to tell them she could not read when she clearly heard old man Eli saying, "*All things be pos'ble with the good Lord.*" She rose slowly to her feet, gently rubbing the top page of the old, worn Bible as she did. A story old man Eli had once shared with them came to her mind; a story about one of the Lord's servants named Peter who had been walking on water but began to sink when he doubted. "Yous mus' have faith, faith in the good Lord," old man Eli had said. "'Cause if yous do, he kan help yous." As Mamie stood there, she realized Peter had not learned to walk on water any more than she had learned to read, yet he had begun to and probably would have made it to the Savior if he had not doubted.

She opened the Bible to the page her thumb was resting and stared at the words. She then felt her mouth moving, "*Ye have heard that it hath been said that thou shalt love thy neighbor and hate thine enemy. But I say unto you, do good to them that hate you and pray for them which despitefully use you and per... perc...persecute you,*" Mamie slowly began as she stared down at the strange words. She felt her eyes leaving the page and found herself looking into the eyes gazing at her. *"Do this that ye may be the children of your Father which is in heaven for he maketh his sun to rise on the evil and on the good and sendeth rain on the just and on the unjust. For if ye love them which love you, what reward have you. Be ye therefore per...perfect even as our Father which is in heaven is perfect."* Silence hung warm and thick in the air as she closed old man Eli's Bible and sat back down.

Something strange, loving, and strong went through Mamie's heart as she sat down with a clear understanding of how Peter could walk on water. She silently thanked the Lord for what she knew he had just done.

The hardships they were suffering were very evident in both songs and words as they stood one by one to share their feelings and their beliefs that they knew the good Lord had not forgotten them.

An older slave man had just finished testifying and they were saying 'amen' when a noise caused them to freeze. Mamie felt herself growing faint as someone stepped from behind the trees and started slowly toward them. From the moans that could be heard around the circle, she was sure the rest of the slaves experienced like feelings. Knowing the worst would soon happen, they watched as the figure of a man got closer and then it became clear; it was a white man.

"Please, dear Lord, have mercy on us," someone cried out.

It was little Solomon who first reached out and took the hand of each person to his sides and slowly the rest of them did the same. Mamie didn't understand Solomon's actions, but she did feel a small sense of comfort even knowing that holding onto each other's hand would not prevent Massa from doing whatever he was surely going to do to them.

"Please, do not fear; I come as your friend," the man said as he continued toward them. His voice made it seem as if the heavens had opened and the good Lord had spoken words of love. Mamie's heart started pounding greatly with joy, for she knew that voice, as did Solomon and others; it was the kind, tall stranger. Solomon rushed forth and the two embraced.

"May I join you?" He asked, looking first at Solomon and then at the rest of them. All heads nodded. He uttered a sincere "Thank you" and sat down by Solomon.

For a few seconds silence hung in the air. Solomon finally started a song and before long, the rest of the slaves were again singing and testifying. The kind, tall stranger clapped his hands with them, but he did not sing. Instead, he sat staring into the fire, his mind seeming to be miles away. Then, unexpectedly, he stood. Mamie, fearing he was going to leave, was about to ask him to please stay when Solomon shook his head to silence her. She then realized he was not leaving but was standing to testify, too.

He cleared his throat, looked down for a second at the ground and then toward the heavens. He looked back down at them and sighed heavily.

"I have watched you and listened to you before," he said. He cleared his throat again and as he did, Mamie's mind quickly traveled back to the first time he had come asking if the slaves would be gathering. The thought that he knew she had lied brought a very sorrowful feeling to her heart, and she asked the good Lord to forgive her.

"I could not stand in the shadows of the trees any longer because my time..." he stopped and looked toward heaven, this time when he looked back at them, his eyes glistened with tears.

"Well, my time and how short it is is not why I am here," he uttered quietly, more to himself than to them. He was silent again but this time they could see he was struggling to control his emotions.

"I have witnessed your trials and tribulations," he finally said. "I have witnessed the beatings you have received; beatings that were so brutal that I'm sure they made our Father in heaven unable to watch, for he loves you the same as he loves all his children. I have also witnessed your hearts breaking as you have pleaded hopelessly each time a love one was taken to be sold as one would sell a horse or plow." His voice had dropped to barely a whisper and it again seemed he was speaking more to himself than to them.

"The cross you bear day in and day out is heavy," he said. He now looked slowly around at them. "But I say to you, be strong and have faith. I have heard many of you speak about Jesus Christ and all he went through, even giving His life for us all. Jesus Christ knew and understood the suffering He would have to go through on this earth, yet He still stepped forward and said, '*Father, send me.*' He was willing to go through whatever sorrows and pains this earth life brought him so that our Heavenly Father's plan might be fulfilled." He paused and again slowly looked around at each of them, his eyes seeming to capture a picture of each one in his mind.

"I believe there were other plans that our Heavenly Father needed to be fulfilled. Like Jesus Christ, who stepped forward, ask yourself if you stepped forward for a plan that would indeed be difficult, but you had enough love to say, 'Father, send me.' My brothers and sisters," he paused and Mamie was glad he did, for her heart was full just hearing him say, '*my brothers and sisters.*' Her heart ached to have Sam and Thomas be there with them and share in this moment. She felt sad as she wondered which one of them had been killed. Trying to remove the sorrowful feeling from her heart, she looked at the kind, tall stranger. As Mamie stared at him now, looking benevolently at Solomon, she knew he was a man who *knew* with all his heart that they were indeed children of God; not just him because he was white and free but also her even though she was colored and a slave. They were *all* His children.

"I say unto each of you, remember the weight of the cross that Jesus Christ had to bear and why you nor I was chosen to bare it. Then think about the weight of the cross you bear and why I was not chosen to bear it. Our Heavenly Father knew that Christ could and would bear the weight of the cross placed upon him. He also knew that you, like Christ, would be strong and endure the weight of the cross placed upon you."

"Please, my brothers and sisters, weep not but endure to the end, and someday, someday you will be crowned with our Heavenly Father's glory for all your suffering. He will continue to lead you; He will continue to guide you, and He will continue to comfort you. He *has not* and *will not* forsake you on this most difficult earthly journey, though at times you might feel he has."

He was silent, this time instead of looking around at them, he stared at the fire, and it seemed for a short time his mind had drifted far away. He looked back up and finally spoke again.

"I have also heard you cry unto the Lord as to 'how long' before your freedom will come; how long must you weep before he hears your cries." He paused, as his eyes moved around the circle to look at each of them. "I say unto you, like waves of an ocean, your freedom *will* roll forth. I promise you, it will roll forth no matter how hard man might try to prevent it. But I also say unto you, ye *will not* be free," he said. His watery eyes looked so very sad as he continued to look around at each of them. "My brothers and sisters, though you will be free, there will still be those who will desire your suffering by denying you most of the rights and privileges they have. There will still be those who cannot enjoy their own self-worth without first demeaning you; who cannot boast of their intellect, unless you are denied an opportunity to learn; who cannot feel strong, unless you are made to look weak." He paused and this time he lowered his eyes to the ground for quite a while, but no one moved a muscle as silence hung thickly in the night air.

"You will have your freedom, but people will still belittle you and your children; they will belittle your skin color, your way of life, the way you talk, your lack of an education, your lack of worldly success, but *you must forgive them.* You must forgive them, for it will become easy for them to forget that for generations you were made to travel the roads less paved or not paved at all. You must forgive them because it will become easy for them to forget that for generations *they* denied you the opportunity to learn; it will become easy for them to forget that you taught yourselves what words you know with no idea of how they were spelled or pronounced. You must forgive them, for it will become easy for them to forget that we are all made in the image of God and to find fault with your looks or skin color is to find fault with Him who made us all. Please, please my brothers and sisters, remember that when we hate our fellow man, we hate God; when we permit others to go hungry, we starve God also; when we deny any man the warmth of our fire, we deny God, too. For God's love is your love, and your love is God's. You must forgive those who mistreat you. You must *forgive* them; you must *weep* for them, *love* them, and *pray* for them, for their earthly joy, as your affliction, shall be but a small moment."

He was silent again as he looked up toward heaven. Mamie sat, completely mesmerized. She looked over at Solomon and then at the rest of the slaves; they too sat motionless except for the frequent wiping away of their tears. There was no mistaking the powerful feeling of love that filled their midst; a love that only the Savior could pour forth.

"My brothers and sisters," he said. "God has restored to this earth the fullness of *His* gospel. Someday you will have an opportunity to receive this great blessing in your free lives if you so chose to accept it. But for a small moment, you will not have this opportunity. I ask of you to *please* have faith; faith that that day will most surely come. Just as your freedom must roll forth, so must the full blessings of the gospel come unto you."

"If I could," he paused as his voice fell to a whisper. "If I could, with my limited knowledge and great love for you, I would surely give unto you all that our Heavenly Father has for all his children. Sometimes it is hard for us to see and understand why certain things must be, yet we must still hold to faith and trust in God and in His love and wisdom. I do seek with all my heart to do *His* will and not the will of man. As His servant, I do not fully understand why certain things must be, but I, too, must exercise great faith in His wisdom and the things He reveals unto me. You, too, must believe in your hearts that He sees the conditions of this world, and all that He does, He does out of love and mercy for us. Let no man make you believe that God loves you less because of the color of your skin or me more because of mine. He is the father of us *all* and His love is just as unconditional and just as equal for each of us."

Pausing, he reached inside his coat pocket and took out a small book. He held it high so that they all could see it.

"Someday, you will read this book. This book, my brothers and sisters, stands as a *second* witness of Jesus Christ. You will know in your hearts that it is indeed the word of God and that by following its teachings you will come to know God's will and plan for you; you will learn how to have God's peace; God's joy. Please, please don't let others trap you into holding onto the past; don't harden your hearts and turn away when the gospel comes to you because it didn't come when *you* or *others* felt it should have come. Remember, the Lord said, '*My thoughts are not your thoughts and neither are your ways my ways. For as the heavens are higher than the earth, so are my ways higher than your ways and my thoughts than your thoughts.*' My brothers and sisters, only God knows the time and the season the gospel will be carried to you, and in His own due time, I guarantee, it shall be. When it does come, I pray He will grant you the wisdom to know that which brings eternal joy." He paused and gently rubbed the cover of the book.

"Please seek out this book, my brothers and sisters. I must be going now, but I can bear you my personal witness that this book contains the Lord's divine gospel and plan for each of you, for each of us. Know of my love for you and my sorrows for your afflictions. Also know always that our Savior loves you and always know that you are never alone, for He will always be with you."

He said a few more words, nodded his head, and then parted from their midst. As he left, so did a heaviness Mamie's heart had been carrying for years. She watched until the stranger could no longer be seen and then she felt her hands slowly opening Eli's old, worn Bible. She looked down and stared at the words her thumb rested near, "A prophet shall the Lord your God raise up unto..." Mamie stopped, stared again in the direction the stranger had vanished and then shook her head and murmured, "Not in this world." She then headed for her shack.

Inside, she thought about the stranger and the things he had said and knew she would miss him wherever he was going, but was thankful for all he had done for her; for them. She asked the Lord to please watch over him wherever he went and thanked Him also for keeping the stranger kind-hearted; that he had not become bad like the other 'good men' they knew. She then committed to the good Lord to someday find that book if He granted her time on this earth to do so. She had no doubt of the truthfulness of the kind, tall stranger's words. She thought about him saying God had other plans and how they had stepped forward for this one. She also felt he had accepted one of God's plans to fulfill on this earth, too, and she felt strongly in her heart that he would.

Mamie could not rest that night. Each time she closed her eyes she would see the book the kind, tall stranger had held up. She wanted that book with all her heart. Even though she could not read, she knew the good Lord would help her to understand the words if she but tried. Old man Eli had once said that if they had a tiny bit of faith, the good Lord could work miracles in their lives. She knew that to be true.

As daylight came, it found Mamie still awake and still very much caught up in what the kind, tall stranger had said. She hoped in her heart that someday he would come again.

I spied him where a fountain burst,
Clear from the rock; his strength was gone.
The heedless water mocked his thirst;

He heard it, saw it hurrying on.
I ran and raised the suff'rer up
Thrice from the stream he drained my cup.
Dipped and returned it running o'er;
I drank and never thirsted more.

Chapter Seven

The Betrayal

The years passed slowly and each carried with it good and painful memories, though the painful ones were most prevalent. Many died over the years; among them was seven year old Isaac. He was bitten by a snake while out trying to pick blackberries and died during the night. Sage also passed away. She was struck by lightening one evening as she sat outside on her porch during a thunderstorm. It seemed like every year took its toll of souls. For Mamie, it took the best of her health and eyesight. Among the good times were the birth of several babies. It was the sound of a little newborn that brought tears of joy that was greater than the sadness of the child's inevitable journey.

As months turned into years the more Mamie's heart felt certain the kind stranger would never be back. She longed for more words of comfort from him, and ever present in her thoughts was the book he had held up. She hungered to know the words within it.

One night during the coldest part of winter Mamie was up late caring for a sick child. The child's head had been burning hot with a fever and she really did not expect him to make it through the night. Then all of a sudden, the fever just went away and the child rested peacefully. Mamie thanked the good Lord as she laid the child on a small straw bed she had made for him next to hers. Her own body ached with tiredness and all she could think of was finally being able to rest. Mamie was about to blow out her small kerosene lamp when a knock came at her door. Since it was very late in the night, she felt certain someone else was ill and needed her help. Preparing to enter out into the cold night air she grabbed the old heavy shawl she had made from the rags of old clothes and wrapped it around her. Before she could get it wrapped completely around her shoulders the knock came again, just as gentle as the first one. Realizing how gentle the knock was, Mamie got the feeling it couldn't be too serious. She opened the door and gasped; there stood the kind, tall stranger.

"I know the hour is late, but yours was the only light I..."

Before he could finish Mamie beckoned him inside from the cold. Once inside he looked at her with wearied eyes.

"If I could just warm my aching, tired feet before I journey on, I would be most grateful," he said. In spite of how happy Mamie was to see him again, it broke her heart to look at him. His eyes had a sad, tormented look in them and reminded her of her son's when he was being taken away to be sold.

As Mamie stared at him, she could not imagine why someone with his good heart would look so downtrodden and alone. She motioned him toward the fire, afraid to speak for fear she would begin to cry. She realized it was almost out and rushed to put another piece of wood on it but had none. Mamie told him she was sorry, but he assured her it was sufficient. As he knelt by the small flames, she took the only quilt she had and placed it on the floor near him.

"Pleas', rest fo' a while," Mamie said, trying to avoid his eyes but unable to do so. The sorrowful look in them was unbearable and the tears she had been fighting to hold back started to fall. She quickly turned to leave, not wanting him to see them. He apparently did, and he called out to her. She stopped, but again couldn't bear to look at him.

"Please," he calmly said, though there was a sound of sadness in his voice. "Please, dear sister, weep not for me. My trials are but for a small moment and then they shall be no more."

Mamie stood still for a few seconds before she turned to look at him and when she did, she no longer saw sorrow in his eyes but peace; a peacefulness that was so beautiful that she felt her own soul being moved to tranquility. She nodded her head and went to rest.

Mamie had no sooner laid beside the child when the thought came that maybe he was hungry. She was about to ask him if he was, but changed her mind as she reminded herself that she barely had enough food to feed the child come morning. She closed her eyes but could not sleep. Mamie knew what she had to do. Getting up, she went over to the old table and poured what little soup she had in one of her old bent cups and carried it over to him.

"I's wish I's had mo' to give yous, s'ur," Mamie said, "but this be all I's have."

He shook his head no and looked down. "I cannot take your last," he said with sincerity.

"Pleas' son, I's like for yous to have it," Mamie said, still holding the cup before him. "The good Lord says that in as much as we's feed the hungr', we's also feeds him. So if yous don't let me give yous this here soup, how kan I's feed the good Lord," she said smiling. He smiled too as he thanked her kindly and took the cup. She turned to go back to rest and again told him to please stay as long as he needed to.

Only when Mamie laid down did she realize she had called him 'son'. She smiled as she thought how kind it had been of him not to be offended that an old slave woman had called him 'son.'

Mamie felt she should get up and try to find out why he was out in the cold so late at night, but she couldn't. Although she had been tired when he arrived, it seemed as if she was all of a sudden overcome with an even more intense tiredness and her eyes soon closed, and she slept. It was a restless sleep though.

Mamie woke several times during the night, and each time she was strangely aware that the small fire was still burning. She was also aware that at one point she saw the kind, tall stranger kneeling, his arms folded, and it looked as if he was praying, his body trembling greatly. She wanted to go to him and speak words of comfort, but her eyes always grew heavy and she would fall back to sleep. The last time she awoke he was finally resting on the old quilt, and she muttered a word of thanks to the good Lord. Strangely though, there appeared to be men around him, but Mamie had a hard time seeing them because the room was so bright. However, even in her drowsy state, she recalled thinking that her fire should not be giving off that much light. She tried to get up and see what was wrong with it, but was unable to keep her eyes opened as she seemed overcome with a desire to sleep.

When morning came, Mamie immediately sat up and looked for the kind, tall stranger, but he was gone. Her heart became very depressed that he had left and she had not said good-bye. She then started recalling the things she had seen during the night and tried to decide if they had happened or if she had dreamed them. She slowly got up and walked over to check the ashes. Every morning, since the fire would burn out soon after she was in bed, there would not be a flame to start another one. Even before Mamie made it to the old hearth, she could see a dim glow in it. She stood there amazed and wondered how such a little fire could still have a dim glow. She then noticed the old quilt she had given the kind stranger to rest on folded neatly on the floor. She smiled, knowing she had not dreamed his being there.

Mamie turned to go check on the child. As she did so, she told herself she had dreamed everything except the kind, tall stranger coming in from the cold.

The child opened his eyes and said he was hungry. Mamie started toward the pot when she suddenly remembered there was no soup left. She was about to tell the child when the thought came to her check the pot anyway. At first she wasn't going to but the thought persisted. Reluctantly, she walked over, tilted the pot nearly upside down, and to her surprise, drops of soup began falling out. She quickly turned it back right side up and grabbed a cup. She tilted it again and watched as drops again slowly began to fall into the cup. They kept coming until she turned it right side up again. She stood there holding a cup full of soup.

"Lord Jesus, thank yous," she said. "Thank yous, Jesus!"

Mamie went somewhat crazy seeing that cup almost filled to the brim when there should have been nothing in it. All of a sudden she just started laughing as if she could not stop. As she laughed, she longed for old man Eli to see what had happened. She knew he would have told her it was indeed a miracle from the good Lord. He had once told them a story about how Jesus had fed a group of five thousand men, women, and children with just two fish and a few loaves of bread and still had some left over. When Eli told them the story, Mamie had not understood how Jesus had fed so many with so little and still had some food left. She had asked old man Eli how it had been done and he said, 'It be a mir'cle child, a mir'cle.'

"Eli," Mamie whispered softly. "I's jus' had a mir'cle in *my* life. Me, a nobody!"

After giving the child the cup of soup, the crazy thought came to Mamie to go try getting some for herself. She went back over and picked up that pot and just looked at it. Then taking another old cup, she held it out and tilted the pot over. Drops started falling *again*. As she watched the cup slowly fill, she just could not stand it any longer. Mamie sat the cup down and stuck her hand inside and rubbed around the bottom of it. It was dry. She tilted it again and nothing came out, not one single drop, even though drops had been coming out when she had stopped. A very dismal feeling came over her as she sat the pot down. She quietly told the Lord she was sorry; she knew in her heart the pot no longer gave because her faith had faltered.

She thought about how old man Eli had talked about how important faith was and so had the kind, tall stranger. She sat down at the old table with a very heavy heart, wishing she could undo what she had done. She then recalled how Peter had doubted and how sad the story had made her feel when old man Eli told it to them. That same sadness now filled her heart except this time it was for her.

The miserable feeling continued as Mamie's thoughts returned to the kind, tall stranger and the look of sadness in his eyes when he had arrived. The more she thought about him, the more she began to wish with all her heart she had been able to stay awake and talk to him. For all he had done for her, she now regretted deeply that she had been unable to forsake her sleep for a small moment.

Mamie went and picked up old man Eli's Bible and sat rubbing its worn pages. As she did, she could almost hear him telling a story about Christ and three of his disciples. It had been a story about how Christ had come to a place called Gethesemane and asked the disciples to sit and watch for him while he went to pray. Eli told how the Savior's heart had been filled with sorrow as he went to pray. Eli had started crying as he told how the disciples had fallen asleep; that they

were unable to stay awake for a small moment *for Christ.*
"Each time Christ return' fro' prayin' thay be 'sleep," Eli said
sadly, shaking his head. He told them that when Christ's time
had come, he again went to his disciples and they were still
asleep. Tears rolled down Mamie's face as she now recalled
old man Eli's exact words. "The Savior said to them '*Sleep on
now, and take your rest; behold, the hour is at hand, and the
Son of man is betrayed into the hands of sinners.*'

As Mamie cried, a very lonely feeling of betrayal tugged
at her heart. At that very moment a horrible chill went through
her and she cried out, "O' dear Lord, pleas', pleas' don't let
anythang ter'ible happen to tha' good man. Pleas' protec' him
from anyone that migh' want to cause him harm. We's need
him, dear Lord."

Stript, wounded, beaten nigh to death,
I found him by the highway side.
I roused his pulse, brought back his breath,
Revived his spirit, and supplied.
But from that hour forgot the smart,
And peace bound up my broken heart.

Chapter Eight

It Is Final

Time continued to slowly pass, and Mamie's thoughts of the kind, tall stranger remained strong. The only change life had brought them was that all the slaves were talking about how the white people were now fighting each other. Stories were often told how a large group of whites had banded together to fight another group. They heard stories of homes being burned, crops being destroyed, and even people being mobbed and killed. Mamie would shake her head and pray for them as she heard more about their fights and destruction.

Although Mamie prayed often for the fighting among the whites to cease, it didn't. It was not until word came that the group most of the whites were against was the group who had once baptized slaves, did she understand.

Mamie's heart grieved for those who were undergoing persecution because of the slaves. She turned her heart to the good Lord and prayed mightily for them. She begged the Lord not to let them suffer for their acts of kindness. But no matter how hard she prayed for them, news of their persecution continued.

One evening, toward the end of June, after getting in from the fields, Mamie and a group of women had gone to the ditch to wash a few rags. She had barely started washing her small load when a cold chill went through her. Looking around, she could see that the other slaves had strange looks on their faces as well. She tried to go back to washing, but the feeling that something awful was going to happen filled her soul.

"Lord hav' me'cy. I's feel somethin' awfa gon' happen," one slave said.

"Maybe Massa gon' sell some of our chilens," another one said.

"I's don't think that be it," someone said to her.

"It be mo' like the feelin' I's get when someone gon' die," another one said. Mamie agreed with her. At that very moment, no one spoke a word as they stared at each other; it was evident they had all gotten the same horrible feeling. They grabbed their few rags and started for their shacks. At first they walked but their pace soon quickened. By the time they reached the shacks they were running as if someone was chasing them. Mamie rushed inside hers and quickly put the old latch on the door, feeling a similar fear to the one she had experienced the night Grace had been killed.

She stood there for a few minutes with her back against the door, very frightened though she didn't know why. There was no Massa outside this time, only a horrible feeling.

Not knowing from where nor when the trouble was coming, Mamie got down on her knees and began praying and pleading with the good Lord to please let whatever it might be, come quickly, for the anxiety of waiting and not knowing was unbearable. That prayer was followed by many more throughout the night as the sorrow in her heart deepened more and more.

Mamie tried to sleep, but whenever she closed her eyes, she saw the face of the kind, tall stranger and saw the same downtrodden look on it as he had had that cold winter night. He looked alone, yet she could see people all around him.

Daylight found her sitting at her old table gravely worried about the kind, tall stranger. She wished with all her heart she knew where he was or had some way of knowing if he was alright.

Mamie was just getting ready to go outside when Solomon stopped by her shack. She could clearly see that he had been crying.

"He won't ever be back, Ms Mamie," he stated with absolute certainty. Mamie felt herself going weak.

"Who?" She asked as fear stirred deep inside her.

"God's friend," he said as he turned with his head down and ran toward the swamps. Mamie wanted to stop him; wanted to learn why but couldn't as all life seemingly drained out of her.

Throughout that day she heard bits and pieces of news from other slaves about a terrible thing that had happened in town. One slave said he had watched the whole thing and told them to meet him that night, and he would tell what he saw.

Mamie felt very restless when they finally gathered to listen to him. She wanted to know, but at the same time something inside feared knowing.

To prolong Mamie's agony, Solomon suggested they sing a song and have her read a scripture before the slave told them his news. She got the feeling Solomon didn't want to face the truth, either. When it came time for her to 'read' a scripture, she stood and silently prayed to the good Lord to guide her to the words he would have her say. She opened the old, worn Bible to a page and stared down at the words for a few seconds. Looking back up, she said, "*Let not your heart be troubled; ye believe in God, believe also in me. In my Father's house are many mansions; if it were not so, I would have told you. I go...*" Her voice and heart broke and she had to fight to hold back the sobs. "*...I go to prepare a place for you.*" She then slowly sat down, feeling the scripture had confirmed her fear that this time he was gone—forever. She looked over at Solomon. He sat with his face buried in his hands as he wept quietly.

The slave slowly and awkwardly began his story. He told them about how angry the people in town had been at a small group of men locked in jail. He said he had looked up as he sat chained outside a store post to see lots of men with faces looking likes theirs rush inside the jail and start firing their guns. Mamie felt her heart grip deeper with fear when he said that. At the same time the crazy thought came to her that the kind, tall stranger was in that jail. She tried to shrug the crazy feeling off as she told herself it could not be; he would never do anything to be in jail. Yet, no matter how hard she tried to shake the feeling, it would not go away. The thought haunted her and made it difficult for her to listen to what the slave was telling them.

"Those shots be ter'ble," he said. "I's kno' tha' whoe'er be in that jail didn't stand a chance to live, but I's pray for them anyway. I's then look' up at the jail window and I's sees a man and I's think I's saw him 'fore. I's not sho'," he said as he tried to control the emotions that were bringing sobs to his throat. Hearing him say this, the thoughts and pictures of the kind, tall man immediately flooded Mamie's mind. This time, instead of fighting the horrible feeling, she began praying.

"No, pleas' dear Lord, pleas' no; pleas' don't let it be him in tha' window," Mamie silently prayed. But the slave telling the story looked directly at her as if he had heard her and began nodding his head.

"Sho 'nough I's think it be him," he continued. "Tha' kind man who talk' to us 'while back 'bout free'om and tha' book. Well, if it be's him, he come to the windo' and thay be shootin' at him. When I's sees him, I cry migh'ily unto the good Lord to help him; I fear' migh'ily for tha' good man. I's fear' thay migh' kill him. I's jus' didn't want anythang to happen to tha' man 'ncase he be tha' kind man. I's also ask' the good Lord to let them kill me and not hurt him cause I's kno'

he be able to help po' people like us mo' than I's be able to.
But when I's look' up at that windo' agin, I's sees him jerk as
if sum'un had hit him in the back. It look like wha'ever happen, made him fall fo'ward. When he did, cause he be so
close to tha' open windo', he falls out. I's sees him fallin' and
I's try to run fo'th in time to get my body 'tween him and the
ground, but those old chains Massa had 'round my ankles be
lock' to the pos', and I's only able to run a few steps. I's feel
so hel'less as I's watch tha' good man hit hard on the ground.
I's drop' to my knees and cry; I's kno' he be dead. I's call..."

Mamie's heart could no longer bear to listen as she stood
and rushed from the group. She walked and walked until her
feet grew tired and sore. Finally she sat down and stared out
into the darkness as she repeatedly asked the stillness of the
night why, why him: what had he done to die so brutally?
Tears that had been held back ever since the horrible feeling
had begun, as an overflowing river that one tries to control,
finally broke free. Her friend and brother was gone; not only
gone but gone possibly believing it was some of *them* who
had done the shooting. She wept openly and loudly: she wept
for him, wept for herself, wept for all the pains those in
bondage had suffered for so many years, and then she wept

because she felt lost and afraid. Finally, she prayed. She pleaded with the good Lord to have somehow blessed the kind, tall stranger to know that slaves had not been the ones at the jail shooting; she prayed for the stranger to have known how much he meant to them; that he would be blessed to know that they would always remember his kindness and politeness to them as his brothers and sisters.

As Mamie finished praying, she again started to cry but only to feel her tears being gently wiped away. In the stillness of that dark and miserable night, she heard the gentle and peaceful words, "*Weep not. Peace I leave with you, my peace I give unto you; not as the world giveth, give I unto you. Let not your heart be troubled.*"

> *In pris'n I saw him next, condemned*
> *To meet a traitor's doom at morn.*
> *The tide of lying tongues I stemmed,*
> *And honored him 'mid shame and scorn.*
> *My friendship's utmost zeal to try,*
> *He asked if I for him would die.*
> *The flesh was weak; my blood ran chill,*
> *But my free spirit cried, "I will!"*

Chapter Nine

Broken Dreams

Mamie was still in the woods when the sun came up the next morning. When she finally made her way to the fields not a word was said. The overseer looked at her strangely but then turned away. Silence hung thickly in the air as they worked. As the hours continued to pass and the sun rose higher and hotter, Solomon began humming aloud. Mamie immediately joined him in an effort to ease the grief within her own heart. Then, as if it had been planned, one by one the other slaves joined in. It was indeed a sound from the heart united as one in an effort to show a tribute of love to the kind, tall stranger.

At first the overseer didn't say or do anything, but as the hours rolled slowly by without a sign in sight that the humming would ever stop, he ordered them the keep quiet. Unfortunately for *him*, his orders did not frighten them, and they continued to hum. Mamie believed every slave there was ready to take any punishment he might inflict upon them, even sacrifice their life, out of respect and a show of love for the kind, tall stranger. Their hearts were full and all the threats in the world could not frighten away the grief they were feeling. Mamie felt a beating, or death, would be a small price to pay for all the kind, tall stranger had done for her. It was evident that Solomon felt the same as he began humming all the louder.

The overseer yelled, "shut up," repeatedly, but to no avail. Finally looking confused and angry, he moved forward and hit the youngest child in the field on the back with his whip, knocking the child to the ground. Solomon raised a hand to silence them, but he continued humming as he stood straight and tall staring at the overseer. Mamie expected the overseer to rush over and strike Solomon. Instead, he did something very strange, he brought up his whip to hit the child again. Seeing this, Solomon immediately stopped humming, but he never took his eyes off the overseer.

"Did one of you darkies die or something?" the overseer asked. When no one answered him, he again immediately brought his whip up as if he was going to strike the child. The slave nearest him started talking. He told the overseer about a white man being killed and how that white man had been a friend to all the slaves. When the slave told him they were all grieving mightily over the kind man's death, the overseer started laughing.

"Well, now don't that just beat all," he said as he sat looking at them as if he could not believe what he had just heard. *"We's all grieving mightily over his being killed!"* the overseer said mockingly and then burst out laughing again. When he stopped he stared at them angrily.

"I'll beat the living daylights out of every one of you if I ever hear such talk around here again," he said as his voice and eyes gave every indication he meant what he said. Slowly they began to work, again Solomon being the last one to start. The overseer looked at him but did nothing. He rode his horse a short distant away then turned and sat staring at them. They were working again, however, Mamie felt certain he knew he had not won any victory; not even a small one.

The spirit of the kind, tall stranger was felt with each and every trial. With the faith and hope given by him, Mamie was able to carry on. She held dear to her heart his words that the good Lord was mindful of the cross they bore day after day.

Mamie's health grew worse and her old eyesight gradually gave way to almost total darkness. The crippled woman passed away and she was given the job of staying and caring for the young children, though she could not see. With the good Lord's help, she somehow managed to make it through each day without bringing harm to those little ones.

One morning as Mamie was rubbing the face of one of the crying babies, someone started pounding forcefully on her shack. All the slaves were in the field. She could not imagine who it was since Massa nor the overseer ever knocked. Before she could find her way over to open the door, the person outside it started shouting her name.

"Ms Mamie, *I's free*; *we's **all** free!*" The voice shouted.

Mamie's heart started pounding; she wasn't sure whether it was pounding with joy or fear. She finally found the door and opened it. As she did she heard the words again. The voice was that of Solomon. From the shaking of her old porch, it was evident he was jumping up and down.

"We's *free*, Ms Mamie, *We's free*," he said as he hugged her tightly.

"What do you's mean, Solomon, we's free?" Mamie asked, her voice and body trembling greatly.

"We's free. We ain't nobod's slave no mo', Ms Mamie. Thank yous good Lord, we's fin'lly free," he said as he started jumping up and down a few more times before finally stopping to hug her tightly again.

"Son, is yous sho'?" She asked, grabbing his arm and squeezing it. Her voice began choking with sobs and her mind recalled the kind, tall stranger telling them they *would* someday be free; free to be baptized without the risk of being beaten.

"Yes, Ms Mamie, it sho' 'nough is. The kind man's words don' come true," Solomon answered, his voice clearly revealing his joy. He started jumping up and down again as Mamie felt the old porch moving under her. She started jumping, too, not high but enough to let the joy running all over her come out. She even turned around and around. "*I's free!*" She whispered to herself.

"Ms. Mamie, 'member the time the kind man said it was gon' hap'en?" Solomon said after they had calmed down for a moment. Mamie nodded her head.

"Yes Solomon, I's 'member," she said solemnly.

"You's didn't b'lieve him, Ms Mamie. But I's kno' he be not lyin' to me; I's kno' he tells me the truth and tha' it be from God. All these years Ms Mamie, I's ne'er forgit tha' he says I's be free someday," Solomon said as if still trying to convince her.

"I's be wrong to doub' him, son. I's be real wrong."

"All these years I's ne'er forgit what he says, and now it don' come true," he repeated and started jumping again.

"Yes son, he sho' did say it would come."

"I's wish he was still here, Ms Mamie. I's wish he could share this good day with us. I's *kno'* he would be real happy, too," Solomon said.

"I's do too, Solomon. I's wish with all my ol' heart tha' he could be here now."

"I's miss him, Ms Mamie. I's miss him for so long, and it not be gittin' any bet'er. I's sho' wish I's could see him agin," Solomon said, his voice sounding very sad.

"Son, I's b'lieve if we's live our lives as the good Lord would have us, we's will see tha' kind man agin and all those peo'le we's not git to see and be with in this life as we's want' to," Mamie said.

"I's hope so, Ms Mamie," Solomon said anxiously.

"Solomon, I's want to find tha' book. I's want to kno' real bad what be in it. I's want to kno' the good Lord's will and plan for me."

"Me too, Ms Mamie. I's gon' to find it, and we's both gon' to kno'. I's mus' be gon' now, Ms Mamie," he said.

"Solomon," Mamie cried out to him as fear started to creep inside her heart. "Wha' do we's do with free'om?"

"Ms Mamie, I's gon' to take my free'om and go git bap'ized. I's wait' a *long* time and now I's gon' to go git it don'. Wha's you's gon' to do with yo's, Ms Mamie?" He asked.

"Free'om means we's kan lea'e Massa, righ'?" Mamie asked him. "It means we's kan go enywhere we's want?"

"It sho' do, Ms Mamie. Massa kant do nothin to us anymo' if we's want to lea'e. We's *free!*" His voice was still filled with excitement and the excitement became all the more intense whenever he said the word 'free.' "So wha' yous gon' do with yo's, Ms Mamie?" He asked again.

"Oh son, I's gon' go and finds my child and tha' book. I's got to finds my child, and I's got to finds tha' book." It was Mamie who was fully starting to feel the full meaning of what freedom meant, and she started jumping around screaming.

All of a sudden, she realized Solomon was not moving. In fact, she noticed that he was being very quiet and still. Slowly she stopped moving and fell silent, too.

"Wha' be's wrong with yous, Solomon?" Mamie asked, sensing something was wrong.

"Ms, Mamie, yous be too old to go lookin' fo' yo' child," Solomon said. "Yous kant see; yous kant har'ly walk. Yous ne'er be able to finds her, or tha' book. Yous be too old to, Ms Mamie. Yo's child mus' finds you." He paused. "Sides, yo's child grow' now; prob'ly got her *own* chilens to find."

Mamie's tears started falling. The things Solomon had said hurt. She knew he was not trying to hurt her or be mean, but his words still hurt her heart deeply. Only her sobs could be heard as they stood in silence for a long time.

"Yous says we's free; yous says we's kan go enywhere," Mamie finally said. "Then wha' good be free'om; wha' good be free'om if I's kant be with my child. I's don't care if she be grow'; she still be my child. Yous asks me wha' I's gon' do with my free'om; I's tells yous but yous acts like Massa and tells me I's be no good for nothin. I's mus' be good for sum'un or the good Lord won't let me be here for free'om. I's gon' find my child, *and* I's gon' find tha' book," she said through her tears. She then slowly turned to go inside. She had barely turned when Solomon grabbed her arm.

"I's sorry, Ms, Mamie," he said, his voice filled with regret. "Yous gots a righ' to do wha' you feels is best to do with yo' free'om jus' as I's got a righ' to do wha' I's want to do with mine."

"Solomon, will you's help me finds my child?" Mamie asked quietly. He apparently didn't hear her.

"I's got to be gon' now, Ms Mamie," he said, and she felt the old porch move as he stepped off it. She did not hear him walking away but after standing there for a moment and not hearing him at all, she knew he must have left. Feeling hurt, she felt her way to the door and went back inside. She found her old chair and sat down. Freedom no longer felt like a blessing.

"I's tell yous wha', Ms Mamie," Solomon's voice rang out again and she realized he had *not* left. "Let me go be bap'ized and I's come back and help yous find yo' child, and then we's find tha' book."

"Solomon, yous means them words; yous gon' help me?"

"Yes, Ms Mamie," he said as he gave her a hug. "Yous jus' stays put and I's promise yous, I's will come back and then we's take yo' free'om and my free'om and go."

"Thank yous, Solomon," Mamie said. "Thank yous. I's want so much to finds her and hears her voice agin and to have and kno' the good Lord's will and plan for me."

"Yous will, Ms Mamie. I's promise yous, yous will. We's won't stop til we's finds her. *I's go now, but I's promise, I's be righ' back real soon.*"

That promise was the last words he said to her before he left, but he never came back. She waited and waited, her heart breaking more and more with each passing hour. She just didn't want to believe Solomon had lied to her.

Late that night one of the slaves awakened Mamie and told her Solomon had been shot and killed while on his way to be baptized. The overseer had been drunk and said he thought it was some wild animal running across the fields; said he had no idea it was a "free darkie."

For days Mamie cried; it was hard to stop the tears as thoughts about how excited Solomon had been when he'd come to tell her freedom had come crossed her mind; his excitement over finally being able to be baptized filled her heart. Being baptized had indeed been the greatest dream freedom had brought him, yet he had not been able to see that one dream come true.

"I's so sorry, Solomon, so very sorry yous didn't make it to be bap'ized after yous be waitin' so long to do so," Mamie said.

Then in a moment to my view
The stranger started from disguise,
The tokens in his hands I knew;
The Savior stood before mine eyes.
He spake, and my poor name he named,
"Of me thou hast not been ashamed.
These deeds shall thy memorial be
Fear not, thou didst them unto me."

Chapter Ten

Dear Savior, Take Me Home

Mamie had no place to go and no way of finding her child. She prayed day and night that the good Lord would not forget her and the hopeless situation she was in, but each passing day left her feeling he had. Feeling the Lord was not going to help her find her way out of this situation, she prayed he would at least grant her enough eyesight so she might find her own way. He did not do that either.

Massa came to see the slaves a few days after they were free. Mamie had feared his coming; she knew he would be happy over finally being able to get rid of her and would now be free to do so. Sure enough, she was right.

"Guess y'all have already heard the news," he said. His voice didn't sound so arrogant and powerful anymore. Mamie wanted with all her heart to be able to see his face. She wondered if he looked as unhappy as he sounded.

"Well I came to tell you I won't be stopping any of you who feel you want to leave. I fe..."

"Yous kant stop us even if yous want' to 'cause we's be free!" Someone shouted out, interrupting whatever Massa was about to say.

"Oh, I *could* stop you if I wanted to; one way or another, nig..." Massa stopped himself. "All I was saying," he continued, his voice very innocuous, "you can stay if you want to. I do need workers to get my crops done and wherever you go, you are going to need work. Since I will no longer be taking care of you, you will need money to live off. I am offering you a job if you want one. You will also have shel..."

"How much yous gon' give us if we's stay and work? I's sho' 'nough won't stay if it be how lit'le yous be's givin' us now," someone shouted.

"First thing you better learn nigger is you don't start talking when *I* am talking; I don't care if you are free; *what ever free is supposed to mean for **you** people*," Massa said. All talking and movements ceased. Massa was still in control.

Mamie raised her hand, hoping she was standing where Massa could see it.

"What do you want Mamie?" he said very coldly.

"I's want' to go finds me's child, Massa, but ol' overseer shoot and kill' Solomon, and he be the one gon' take me. I's got no place to go Massa, so I's stay and work yo' crops. I's be willin' to take wha'ever pay yous gives m..."

"My offer does not include you Mamie. I would be a fool to keep you here when you can't see. Can't waste my money on the likes of you," Massa said.

Mamie stood there a moment feeling totally humiliated and less than the dirt underneath her feet. Feeling greatly ashamed and hurt by his words, she fought desperately not to cry, but the tears started rolling down her face anyway. Realizing she could not hold them back, she slowly turned to leave, though she didn't know the exact direction of her shack. She had only taken a few steps when she felt the ground drop from underneath her next step and she crashed hard against it, face first. Frightened, she started pleading for someone to help her, though the words were hardly out when she felt hands helping her up.

"Look at you, Mamie; you can't even help *yourself* and you want to work for me. You get your things and get off my land unless you can pay me to stay on it. If the rest of you who can give me a good honest day's work want to earn some money before you go, you can stay," Massa said, his voice sounding extremely frustrated. "I will..."

"Massa," Mamie yelled. "Yous think yous be bet'er than me cause yous kan see and yous got land and all, but yous be nothin without me and the rest of these here slaves. *Nothin'!* She paused. "And yes, I's inte'rupted yous and yo' hol'ow words. Eny slave tha' stays and works for *the likes of yous* be real crazy, *even* a blind one like me. Now someone git me to my shack 'fore I's take a notion to throw up all over yous, Massa."

Someone took Mamie's arm and said they'd help her to her shack. She nodded okay, though she longed to be able to do it proudly by herself. For the first time in her life she felt like someone; not an '*animal*' as they'd been termed by Massa and others like him, but a *human being*, and with that feeling, she felt *dignity* .

Being old and blind was a terrible feeling, but even worse was being alone. Though Massa had told Mamie to leave, she had nowhere to go. Day after day she sat in her shack, alone and afraid. She knew that eventually Massa would come and throw her off his land if she did not go freely. She found herself wishing the good Lord would have taken her a long time ago. It just didn't seem right to be old, alone, and have nothing and no one. She was now free to go out into the world with absolutely nothing to show for all those hard years of work, nothing except the scars of slavery.

Mamie began to cry as she thought about having nothing. She asked the good Lord why he didn't at least let her keep her sight. She told him she just could not understand him leaving her alone and in total darkness.

Mamie's own sorrowful situation was forgotten for a small moment when she received news that a small slave boy was missing. Mamie felt her way outside and stood on her old porch and listened to discussions about the small boy. The boy's mother, seeing Mamie, rushed forth and embraced her. Mamie held her close and let the mother's sobs mix with her own. How she longed to have her eyesight and be more useful. The mother was soon lead away, but promised Mamie she would let her know if and when they found the child. Soon the place was quite as everyone joined in the search, most feeling certain they should search around the swamp first. Making her way back inside her shack, Mamie felt a deep feeling of hopelessness as she longed to join the search.

Feeling lost and frustrated, she began to talk to old man Eli aloud even though she knew he was gone and could not hear her. "Yous lied to me, Eli," she said. "Yous lied when yous tells us that story 'bout the good Lord restorin' that blind man's sigh' or when he heal' that woman from that disease she had suffer' with for years. Yous lied and I's kno' now yous lie 'cause the Lord ain't help' me with my sigh' and I's done begg' and begg' him to. If yous tells the truth Eli, why he helps them and not helps me? Why Eli?"

In spite of how loud she was talking and sobbing, she heard the voice of the kind, tall stranger say, "*Have faith; please have faith. The Lord has not forgotten you, nor forsaken you.*"

Mamie stopped sobbing and remained very still.

"Is tha' yous sur?" Mamie cried out, her heart pounding with a mixture of hope and doubt. Not getting a reply, Mamie rested her head against the back of her old chair.

"I's not only old, I's crazy, too," she said aloud.

It seemed like an eternity before Mamie finally heard a gentle knock on her door. "Dear Lord, pleas' do't let it be's bad news," she prayed silently as she made her way toward the door. As she moved forward, Mamie again longed for her eyesight. Her heart gripped with fear as she slowly opened the door.

"We's find him, Ms Mamie. We's find my baby," the voice of the mother cried out joyously as she hugged Mamie. She then told Mamie what the boy had told them on the way back to their shack. Mamie listened intently as the mother told her how the boy had awakened hungry and decided to go to the water bank where they did washing and try to catch some fish with his hands. He had wondered too far out and found himself sinking. The last thing he recalls was screaming as his body went farther down into the water.

"I's tell you Ms. Mamie, that white man saved my baby lif'. My baby say he kno' he be's dea' if tha' white man hadna' sav' him." Mamie could feel the mother's tears fall onto the side of face as she hugged her again, but Mamie's heart seemed to have stopped beating as she clinched the mother's arm.

"The man," Mamie gasped, her heart pounding greatly. "Please, tell me 'bout tha' man; who he be?"

"I's not kno', Ms Mamie, but when we saw him gen'ly car'ing my son t'ward us, I's just run screamin' to git my baby. He's leav' 'fore I's could thank him. He's jus' se'm to dis'pill. My baby say he's be rea' kin' to him. He's ev'n wrap'd my's baby in his own coa'; let him keep it, too. I's got to go now, Ms. Mamie. I's gon' go hol' my chil' and nev' let him fro' me agin." With that she rushed off. Mamie called out to her to please tell her more about the white man, but her words got no reply.

"Good Lord, could it be's him; was it my kin' frien'?" She quietly whispered to herself as she slowly closed her door. Her heart reminded her that he had died a long time ago. Sitting down, she found herself reflecting back to the words of the slave who had witnessed the kind stranger's death. She sought to find something in his words that maybe the kind stranger could still be alive.

"I's rea'ly crazy," she said, convinced that maybe he could be alive since the slave had said he wasn't sure it was the kind stranger.

Mamie slept peacefully that night and for a few more, but gradually the peaceful feeling wore off and day after day she would sit rocking back and forth, with a few rags and Eli's old Bible tied in a small bundle, listening to the place become quieter and quieter and knowing that most of the slaves had taken what little they had and left. No one stopped by to say good-bye. She felt it was because they didn't want to see the look on her face or feel any guilt in leaving her behind. Before long, the place was completely quiet. Terror filled Mamie's heart; they had *all* left, all but her.

Mamie didn't cry anymore; she didn't hope anymore; she didn't pray anymore. She simply didn't care anymore. She had had enough of life's trials and pains. She just wanted to rest from it all.

It didn't take long for her to realize her time had come when she heard the sound of someone approaching a few days later. She knew it would be Massa, but she felt no fear. In fact, she was glad it was about to all be over.

Mamie's porch made a loud creaking sound as the person stepped onto it. She then heard her door slowly open. She almost smiled as she thought about how Massa was hoping he would open it and find her gone. It continued opening until she was certain she was in full view. He didn't say a word and neither did she as she sensed him standing in her doorway.

"I's don't care what yous do to me anymo' Massa," Mamie finally said.

No answer or movement.

"Massa?"

No answer. Mamie waited a few seconds before she spoke again.

"Who's be there?" She asked, her heart starting to pound with fear.

"It be me, and I's come fo' yous," a voice said, and it definitely was not Massa's or the overseer's or anyone white. Mamie's heart started pounding greatly with hope.

"Who be yous?" She asked, not wanting to believe what her old ears had heard.

Someone then took one of her hands and placed something in it. As she slowly rubbed the object and the string attached to it, her heart started beating with joy. It was a wood chip!